FOUR DUCKS ON A POND

A HIGHLAND MEMORY

NICHOLAS THE CAT

with Annabel Carothers

Illustrations by LYN DUNACHIE

First published in 2010 by
Birlinn Limited
West Newington House
10 Newington Road
Edinburgh
EH9 1QS

www.birlinn.co.uk

ISBN: 978 1 84158 876 6

British Library Cataloguing-in-Publication Data
A catalogue record for this book is available
from the British Library

Designed and typeset by Mark Blackadder

Printed and bound in Great Britain by Bell & Bain Ltd., Glasgow

Puddy with Carla and Nicholas

Fionna and Grandpop outside the old henhouse

CHAPTER ONE

Nobody could call me inquisitive, but because I am quiet and unobtrusive I observe much and ponder deeply. And so I have decided to write down what I have seen and known of my family, those humans and animals who live in, or around, this sturdy granite building we share as our home.

There was a time when this house was a manse, but the minister was in charge of a church nearly two miles away and not of that one beside the loch, just across the road. This must have been an inconvenient arrangement, but people have a way of making difficulties for themselves. Near the church is the old smithy, now a ruin, and close to it is the school and the teacher's house. These are our nearest neighbours. The village is a mile away, and there are cottages dotted here and there, but mostly these are ruins. The church belonging to the manse, when it was a manse, is now a byre. So you will know that we live in a desolate place, and where there were fields of corn, now there are fields of bracken, or there are stretches of heather, interspersed with white warning flags of bog-cotton, since here is a land which man has never hoped to cultivate. There are hills around the loch, and in patches stunted trees, all with a slant towards the east, for the westerly winds blow relentlessly, and the trees bear this mark of their surrender.

On the loch are five tiny islands, the nesting place of many birds, and there are rushes on the loch and delicious white foam. Often the water is grey and angry, and the foam forms stripes across, which is a sign of worse to come. I hear Grandpop say, 'The loch is stripy. It's going to rain.' And it does. But the loch can be blue, oh so blue that to paint it would seem like a coloured lie, or it is a mirror reflecting perfectly the hills and the scrubby trees and rushes and the tiny granite church. And so it was now, as I sat on the wall, and I gazed and dreamed, and I thanked God that I had a smart white shirt and black shoes and a multi-coloured coat. I thanked God for where I was, for this is a wonderful place, and the grasshoppers chirped and the rabbits frolicked (for they had not seen me, since the lichen-coloured stones of which the wall is built are remarkably like my coat). And all the time in the background was the soporific murmur of the sea.

Presently the mail bus would pass along the winding road. Sometimes it stops at our gate, but we are not expecting a guest today, and all of the family are in the house, so it would go past, on to the village, and the village people would be gathered round the post office, less to collect letters than to see who was coming off the bus, and why. Unlike me, these people have a great curiosity. But I learn more than they do by just being quiet. I heard the bus now, away in the distance, for it was deadly still and sound carried far. As it came in sight I saw first its white top, then its crimson-painted body, and I knew by the labouring sound of the engine that it was the old bus, the small one, for it was too early in the year for the big bus to be out. The tourist season had not yet started. When it did there were sometimes four buses on the road, in convoy, and nearly everyone in them would be going to Iona, though why they cross the ferry to that place when they could stay here is one of my big puzzles.

To my surprise, the bus stopped at our gate after all, and Neilachan, the driver, climbed from his seat and placed a cardboard box beside our gate. The curious thing was that the box was twittering and cheeping. Neilachan sounded his horn to draw attention, and grinding the gears (because it was an old bus) he drove on. Nobody came from the house.

Kitten would be in the kitchen preparing supper, and Margie would be chatting to her. Grandpop was making a new hen house at the back, so I expected Fionna and Puddy and Buddy were there, helping. Carla would be where Puddy was. I worked this out in my mind and sauntered over to the box. Yes, it chirped and twittered, and I knew what it was. The day-old chicks had come, and they were white Leghorns, because our Rhode Island Reds were so broody. I stopped to titivate my white shirt, while I debated whether or not to tell the family that the bus had been. While I was still thinking, I heard Fionna's bicycle bell, and she came hurtling down the drive, calling over her shoulder, 'John, it's the chicks!' John is Buddy. Some call him one thing, some the other. It is the same with the rest of the family. They each answer to several different names, but they always call me Nicholas or Nicky, which is nonsense, as my real name is Nathanial. But they don't know, so I let it pass.

John appeared from the back of the house. He always wears a kilt when he's here, and very good he looks in it too, being tough and broad-shouldered, though not very tall. His blue short-sleeved shirt matched his eyes, and his curls stood up on end, so I know he had been very busy. He smooths down his curls when he can, pretending they aren't there.

By the time he reached Fionna she had opened the lid of the box, and I could see a moving mass of yellow fluff.

'Any dead?' John asked.

'None. And I think they've sent twenty.' Fionna put back the lid and picked up the box.

'Jolly O,' said John. He often said this and it meant he was pleased. 'Mummy's lighted the brooder. It's in the cottage. Take them to her.'

Fionna went up the drive, and John sighed and picked up her bicycle, which she had left lying on the ground. Then he saw me.

'Nicholas, the Liddle Cat!' he said, in the silly voice he adopts for me. 'Where have you been, you old spiv? Killing bunnies for the Black Market?'

I busied myself cleaning my shirt. This stupid talk

annoyed me. As I am a good and energetic hunter, can I be blamed for selling the surplus, each at a price others are foolish enough to pay? And of course humans don't understand our currency any more than we understand theirs.

John put his hand under my tummy and scooped me up, placing me gently in the bicycle basket. I liked the feeling of his hand against me, and my hurt pride was quickly soothed. I stood on tiptoe in the basket and rubbed my head against John's hand as he wheeled me up the drive.

'Fecky cat.' John said, leaning the bicycle against the garage doors. I purred loudly, hoping he would stay with me a little while, but he dumped me on the ground and gave me a light playful prod with his foot. 'Come and see the baby chickens.' He said. 'And remember they aren't for you.'

The cottage is near the back door of the house. It used to be occupied by the servants, but for years now there have been no servants, so it has become a dump for all the surplus stuff from the house and for the outworn toys and treasures of the family.

I tripped carefully after John along the cinder track leading to the little green door with the painted horseshoe nailed over it, upside down, so that the luck would not run out. Puddy and Fionna, and Carla, were peering at the new chicks huddled behind the wire netting Grandpop had fixed around the little cone-shaped brooder. Carla whimpered a little, her tail wagging and her whole body quivering. Her long black

ears hung down her blue roan back, and her brown
liquid eyes seemed to me to flicker with a desire which
I hoped Puddy would notice, before it was too late.
Puddy seemed to read my thoughts.

'If you touch the chickens, I'll beat you, Carla,' she
said. Carla is always being threatened with a beating
but she's never had one yet.

'Can the chickens find their way home?' Fionna
asked, but nobody heard her, for John and Puddy were
arguing about the temperature of the brooder.

'The book says ninety degrees,' John said.

'But if it's ninety without the chickens in it, it will
suffocate them when they pack in and we shut the
door,' Puddy answered, which I consider was a sensible
thought.

'Chickens can stand any amount of heat. It's chills
that kill them,' John said, crumbling some oatmeal
between his finger and thumb and sprinkling it among
the chicks. They already had a little trough of oatmeal,
a dish of milk and a dish of water, so any extra tit-bits
were quite unnecessary. Anyhow, they appeared to
prefer the powdered peat with which their run was
littered and were scraping away vigorously as if they'd
lived for years instead of for a few hours. Presently a
bluebottle caught my eye. It was buzzing wrathfully
against the back window, the one that overlooks the
hen run. I jumped onto a pile of books stacked in the
windowsill. At some time or another I had read all of
these books. *Hobbies Annual* (with love to Buddy,
Christmas 1928), *Sonnenschein's Latin Grammar* (with

scribbles all over it and 'Form this' and 'Form that' in Roman lettering), *Palgrave's Golden Treasury* and several 'Verity' editions of Shakespeare, all very inky.

Beside me was the creaky revolving bookcase containing the *Encyclopaedia Britannica*, year 1882. This, I confess, I have not read entirely.

I could see a huge spider waiting for the bluebottle and decided to let him capture it. I preferred to watch the hens, ten of them, all Rhode Island Reds, cared for by a Light Sussex cock who was named Geraldo, after the famous band leader. He was very attentive to his hens and had immaculate manners.

Presently I realised that the family had gone and, not noticing me, had shut me in the cottage. There are disadvantages in being so quiet. However, I had had a good meal not long ago, and after I watched the spider parcelling up the bluebottle, I settled down for a nap, tucking my paws under my chest in the way John says makes me look like a sphinx. But he's wrong, for I've never seen a sphinx with tucked-in paws. And I've seen most things.

As I suspected, the day-old chicks soon brought Puddy back. She is one of those people who worries a lot and imagines all sorts of dreadful things happening, so she makes sure she is around to see that they don't. She made twittering noises, which the chickens ignored, and, opening the cone lid of the brooder, she adjusted the flame of the little paraffin lamp. I don't know whether she turned it up or down. Up, probably, because of what John had said about the chills.

I jumped lightly off the windowsill and rubbed myself against her leg.

'Darling Nicky,' she said absently, picking me up, 'sly old cat, lurking round the brooder.' But I knew she knew that I would not touch her chickens. I never even touch birds, because I know she loves them. John's right. I'm an affectionate cat and I like to please.

There was a soft click-click outside, and Puddy quickly shut the cottage door. Unfortunately for them, but luckily for the family, the goats have knees that click when they walk. Otherwise they could creep up and do all manner of damage without attracting notice. There are two goats, Flora and Arnish. They are British Sanaan, white, and hornless, and Arnish is bigger and older than Flora, so it is a pity that she belongs to a library which supplies her with subversive literature, for Flora is easily impressed.

Goodness knows what Arnish tells her in the quiet of their home, the little wooden house at the end of the barn, opposite the cottage.

We heard the clatter of little hooves as the goats pawed at the door, and presently their wise, inquisitive faces appeared at the window. Puddy, who had been stroking my ears as she contemplated the chickens, giggled and went to the window. Flora and Arnish were chewing, as usual, their white beards bobbing in the fading light.

'Go to bed, I'm coming to milk you,' Puddy told them, 'and I'll expect a lot of milk, after all the damage you've done today.' There had been a commotion that morning, something about the potatoes John had left in the garage, ready for planting, and he'd left the garage door open. So of course the goats had taken advantage of the situation, since nobody was around to hear their knees, and they had eaten some of the cushions from the dog-cart for good measure.

Satisfied that the chickens were all right, we left the cottage and found the goats having a butting match over a piece of rag. Arnish always won these matches, rising on her hind legs and diving down on Flora in a manner that was most graceful. Puddy didn't try to stop them. She knew that they never did one another any harm.

We went out by the small side gate, across the wild heathery bit called the Dalvan, and so to the big field over the road, always called 'The Fence', where Peter and Iain, the year-old bullocks, lived. Peter and Iain were new to the family, having been bought by Puddy at the local auction sale only a few days before, and we had to watch them in case they returned to their old home, a farm not far away. Peter was half Highland, half Galloway, dark brown with a white tummy. Iain was almost entirely Highland, rather shaggy, and the beautiful horns so typical of his breed had been removed by a vet, perhaps luckily for us, but aesthetically a pity. Both of the bullocks came up to the big white gate and allowed Puddy to stroke them. I wriggled out of her arms and walked slowly a little way away, not because I was afraid but because I thought it right that, while she was cultivating their friendship,

Puddy should be able to give Peter and Iain her undivided attention. She must have appreciated this, for when she had done talking to them, she came over to me and picked me up and carried me back to the house, whispering nice things about me all the while.

We entered the house by the back door. Kitten was stirring something on the Aga cooker, and Fionna was beside her, scraping a pot with a spoon and eating the scrapings. I guessed Kitten had been making fudge. I knew by the flickering in the hall that Margie was lighting the lamps, and from the little back sitting-room, crackling noises meant that Grandpop was stoking up the fire. The gurgling of water outside the back door combined with the heartening sound of a rich baritone voice singing 'Over the Sea to Skye' told me John was just out of his bath.

The cosy family evening was about to begin, with Puddy stealing the soup, which I'm afraid is the only way to describe her repeated tasting of it, and Carla eyeing my empty dish on the table, just as if I had been fed and she had been forgotten. There was a pleasant sameness about our evenings which someone less discerning than myself might consider dull. But I had already discovered that it is the small things in life that matter. The big things have a way of becoming nothing but a mark in time from which the small things are measured.

And so it these small things that I am remembering and writing down before I get too old to remember anything at all.

CHAPTER TWO

Last night was one of my unlucky nights. There was a gale warning for Sea Area Malin (which is us) announced during the variety programme the family was listening to on the radio. So when Grandpop came into the kitchen to stoke the Aga before going to bed, he saw me lying in the big kitchen chair and said, 'Poor little Nicky, you must sleep indoors tonight.'

Now, I know he meant it well, and I know that even on good nights the family worry about me being out on my own, but they are dreadfully, dreadfully wrong. And

Corrie and Arnish

as I can't tell them how much I enjoy outside, I just have to slip off when they let Carla out for her last run, and usually I manage it unless, like tonight, I am caught napping.

Since I wasn't going to get out for the night, at least I might wangle a little extra milk. I sat up in the chair, tilted back my head and opened my mouth wide in the silent 'meow' which I know always melts Grandpop's heart.

'Poor little Nicky,' said Grandpop again, and he walked with his slow, heavy tread across the kitchen into the pantry, where Puddy kept the goats' milk in huge bowls to collect the cream. Grandpop has not got a beard, or anything as ancient as that, but his back is very bent because he has arthritis. He was a very great doctor in his time. A pity he didn't do something about his back. I would have.

He poured my milk out of a jug so as not to disturb Puddy's cream and placed my dish on the little table by the kitchen window. This is where they feed me, so that Carla cannot reach. Carla was still outside, and I guessed she had probably found something disgusting to eat. Let me say here and now that Carla is very grand, with a pedigree longer than my tail, and she comes from kennels just outside London where they breed the most famous cocker spaniels in the world. But she has shocking lapses in taste and eats the skin and entrails of rabbits that I have discarded, and all manner of muck besides. I've even seen her eating with the hens, a thing no self-respecting cat would do.

I make no bones about who I am. I was bought for seven and sixpence from a pet shop in a suburb of London called Ealing, but I am, and always have been, very fastidious. You will think it is a far cry from Ealing to the Isle of Mull, and how on earth did I get here? So I'll tell you. Margie brought me here in a basket when I was only a kitten, but I assure you I have not forgotten my friends and relations in the outskirts of the Metropolis (doesn't that sound better than the suburbs?), and I correspond with them enough to avoid being insular. Besides, when one is in business, one needs contacts, though don't think my motives are entirely mercenary.

Margie has a very important position in a film studio near the pet shop. She has had a big operation so she is home for some weeks, but usually she comes only for the summer holidays and for Christmas and Easter besides. When she arrived home, her face was very grey and she could hardly walk, and it made me very sad to see her like that. But already she is better, and every day I go out with her when she sets fire to the dead grass and rushes that clutter up the fields. The bending and stretching involved is good exercise for somebody who has had an operation. You may find this a useful hint if ever you have one, though of course I hope you won't.

Carla came rushing back into the kitchen, licking her lips and looking very pleased with herself. Grandpop had not noticed how long she had been out, as he was putting ashes in the tray he thoughtfully leaves for me when I have to spend the night at home. Carla sat very bolt upright, just under me. Her sharp sense of smell must have informed her that all I had had was milk, which normally she won't touch, but she likes to sit there, staring at me as I drink, hoping to make me discomfited. In many ways Carla and I are the best of friends; often I share her bed and sometimes even her feeding-bowl, but I cannot deny that she has some nasty traits and can act in a very tiresome and petty way. And I hope that observation is not unkind.

Puddy came into the kitchen and, taking the big torch-lantern from the dresser, went outside, and I could see by the trail of light that she went into the cottage. Presently she came back, carrying the brooder, which of course was all shut up now for the night. I could hear Grandpop in the back porch going 'Hum, hum, hum' and Puddy's voice raised in explanation – the chicks would be better in the kitchen for the first few nights to make sure that they would be all right, even if the brooder lamp went out. Poor Puddy, she does picture every sort of disaster! I could tell by Grandpop's 'hum-hums' that he thought she was fussing, and frankly so did I. But she put the brooder on the red table beside the Agamatic boiler, and I hoped she'd sleep the better for knowing it was there.

Now John came in, and said he was hungry and wanted FOOD – I've printed it big, just like he says it. This simple statement was followed by a wild dance, with leaps in the air and clicking of heels, which John alone can execute, and which, he says, is his Russian dance. The noise he made of course brought Kitten and Fionna into the kitchen. Kitten is not related to me. She is married to Grandpop, and this is her pet-name, something to do with the Gaelic for dearest, for Kitten belongs to this house and always has done, and that's why the family lives here. She is still very beautiful, although her inky black hair is now streaked with grey, and she is very temperamental, like all good Highlanders. Fionna says she is disappointing as a granny because she doesn't wear a bonnet and shawl, but Fionna also allows that there's something to be said for an old lady being slim and smart and agile, and able to do Highland dancing steps or a funny dance she calls her Fairy Dance, kept usually for birthdays or Christmas or to cheer up someone who is ill.

Of course, when Kitten heard John wanted FOOD she got busy with the kettle and the bread-knife, although it was bedtime, and Grandpop was standing there looking at his watch and hum-humming about getting up in the morning.

Margie was already in bed. She still went early, but I knew she would want to eat whatever the others were having, and, sure enough, Fionna began to lay the tray with six cups and saucers. I say 'began', for Fionna rarely finishes anything. She says something she wants to say, and by the time she's said it, she's wandered off and forgotten what she was doing. She's at the age when children can't talk without climbing absently about the furniture, or hugging whoever she is addressing and wanting to get round. Fionna is getting tall, but is slim and neat, when she is tidy, which is not often. Her chestnut hair is straight and straggly round her shoulders, and her eyes are the colour of peat. She has a slow, purring voice, and a wee bit of a Highland accent, which she gets from Kitten. She has a beautiful nature, which Puddy says she gets from her father. Fionna's father is the man in the photograph on Puddy's dressing-table. He is wearing uniform and medals and a badge with a world and a laurel leaf round it. Once a year, for a few days, Puddy fixes a poppy to the picture frame. Puddy is Fionna's mummy. She is not a 'puddy' now, but she was when she was a little girl. She is not much bigger than Fionna, and has fair hair, usually wind-blown, and green-brown eyes, and she's the one who mostly looks after us all. As I've said before, she worries a lot, and John says she's very obstinate.

I think I've managed to tell you something of all the people inside this house, though there's not been much about Margie. That's because, being ill, she is still a bit shadowy, but you'll know more about her later. She is Puddy's sister, and of course John's as well, and Fionna calls her Aunt. She has dark hair and big blue eyes, and she has never married, because she didn't want to, not because she couldn't. And that, as you know very well, makes all the difference.

Puddy had finished laying the tray, and Kitten was making the tea, while John cut hunks of bread and sloshed home-made butter and jam onto them. If anyone else did it like that, the result would be crude, but John has a knack of making anything he touches look appetising. I didn't follow them upstairs, as I felt that Carla was in a bouncy mood, so I'd best avoid her. As soon as the creaking on the stair stopped, I knew they were safely in Margie's bedroom, and I slipped over to Carla's bed, which lives in an alcove in the scullery, where there are hot pipes, so it is very cosy. And there, believe it or not (as Grandpop would say), I stayed all night because nobody noticed me when they came downstairs to wash up, and Carla was willing to have me curled up beside her. It's a lucky thing that Puddy came down very early in the morning to look at her chickens, because I had forgotten that Grandpop's tray of ashes had been left in the back-porch, and there was the scullery door and the kitchen door between me and it when I woke up. But Puddy arrived just in time, and I was able to go out with Carla, which is much better. Nobody would punish me for what they knew was not my fault, but all the same, I am an affectionate cat and I like to please.

And here I come to the last member of the family. The last of all I mean, and not just the indoor ones. And this is the 'piece to resistance' (I learnt that phrase from Heath's *Modern French Grammar* in the cottage) for this is my very best friend. She was waiting for me at the back door, as Puddy always opened the paddock gate when there was a gale-warning so that the house could be used for shelter if required. Her breath came steamily from her nostrils in the cold morning air, and there was patience and affection in her kindly eyes. She moved very delicately as I stepped from the house because, being big and heavy, she is careful never to risk hurting me with a clumsy step. Yes, she is Corrieshellach, our Highland pony, silver dun, and thirteen hands three inches high. She greeted me with the low, Highland whinny that had first endeared her to me, and when I had done what I so urgently needed to do, I went with her round the end of the barn to the cosy spot she had been in all night, carefully out of the way of the wind. And she lay down slowly, ponderously, and shook her mane so that it lay in silvery streamers over her neck. And I climbed up on her and nestled against her, and closed my eyes, but took care to purr rapturously into her listening ear.

So now you know why I like to be out at night – to see the things that interest me and to end up with my friend, who, of the whole family, is to me the dearest of all.

CHAPTER THREE

The night had not been so stormy as we had expected. Of course, we so often have gale warnings that we don't much bother about the gales when they come, unless the force of the wind is so great that it tears off the ridging from the house or barn and hurls it across the fields, or sucks the doors from the out-houses, or overturns the wheelbarrow, or whips the milking-stool from its place by the goat-house and carries it through the sky like a kite. All this happens, and often, but not

Corrie, Fionna and the dog-cart

last night. By daylight, the haystacks were still standing, and the big gate John had made for the big field, which was always the first to blow down, was still in its place.

I lay quietly on Corrieshellach's shoulder, which rose and fell slowly as she breathed. It was deadly calm again, as it had been yesterday evening, and I could hear Puddy moving about in the scullery, making the morning tea, which presently she would take upstairs to the rest of the family. It was over an hour since she had come downstairs, but that was because of the chickens, and she would not want to wake the family so soon. She would have spent that hour sitting by the Aga, with Carla on her knee, and sometimes she would doze off, and sometimes tickle Carla's ears. I knew, because once I had watched her through the window.

'Nathaniel!' Corrieshellach's low voice startled me. She went on – 'Nathaniel, I've chust been dreaming about John, and I do not like my dream at all. No, not at all.'

I must tell you that Corrieshellach is Gaelic-speaking so that her English, such as it is, is very pure, very soft, and very carefully said.

'I saw a letter come to the house, and then boxes leave, and goodbyes said. And John left the house, and by car too – not in the bus.' She sighed. 'I do not like it. Not at all.'

Like so many Highlanders, Corrieshellach has the second sight, so her words chilled me considerably.

'Och, he'll be going for a visit,' I said sharply. I

wanted to convince myself, as well as Corrie. And I put in the 'Och' to make me feel a wee bit Highland too. I can do that with Corrie, because she never teases me about the trace of cockney accent I somehow can't altogether lose.

Later in the day I began to feel that it was nonsense to worry over Corrie's dreams. The family had been as usual at breakfast, sitting round the kitchen table, which was covered with a brightly coloured checked cloth. The family always had breakfast in the kitchen, to save labour. I don't know why they don't save labour by eating there all the time, but people are funny that way.

As they ate they argued about the endless topics they find to argue about, while bacon and eggs sizzled and spat in the pan on the Aga, ready to be served directly the porridge was eaten. Puddy had been late for breakfast as she'd had the chickens to feed as well as the hens to see to and the goats to milk. But she didn't eat porridge, so that was all right. I knew, too, that she'd taken oats in a bucket to the big field, so that Corrieshellach would go in there, and the gate would be shut on her, to keep her from hanging round the kitchen door all day. I had often warned her not to be enticed with oats, but she was so greedy that she'd rather follow them to the field than have the endless snacks of bread and potatoes that came her way if she stayed near the house.

After breakfast everyone had routine jobs to do. Kitten washed up, Fionna helped to clear the table, Puddy raked out and stoked the Aga and Agamatic,

Grandpop went hum-humming off to his workshop, to do goodness knows what, and John went up to Margie's room to collect her tray. He took a long time about this, as he would smoke a cigarette and listen to 'Housewives' Choice' with with her before he brought down the tray to Kitten (who would have finished washing up by then). He would then go out and continue making the new hen-house.

A lot of cleaning goes on in the house every day. I often wonder if it is really necessary, and why the family are so fussy about it, for I have often noticed that they are not so clean in their persons as I am. I wash myself thoroughly at least four times a day, but except for their hands, I don't think they wash more than twice.

Carla of course brings a great deal of mud into the house, as she follows Puddy out to collect the coke and throw away the ashes, and as it is so often wet outside, Carla's very feathery paws splodge a route of mud through the kitchen. Then Kitten gets cross and says why doesn't Puddy leave Carla indoors? Puddy tries to do this, and Carla yowls until she has to be let out. And so it goes on, day after day.

A word about Carla's feathers. You may think, as I used to do, that feathers belonged only to birds, but I've learnt that the long fluffy hair on a spaniel's legs are called feathers too. Whether or not the same is the case in other breeds, I couldn't tell you.

Margie arrived downstairs in time to make the coffee and sandwiches, which is all the family have for lunch. Sometimes she uses fish-paste, which I have a liking for, so I would sit quietly, with my tail tucked neatly round me, waiting for the scraps she was sure to throw me. But today was not one of those days, as she used Gentleman's Relish, which should count as fish, but in my opinion doesn't. It is very grand and expensive, but I don't care for it as it is much too salted. I therefore set out to catch myself a rabbit, and I noticed, as I left the house, that Puddy was bringing the dog-cart harness from the cottage, where it was kept. That meant that after lunch she would harness Corrieshellach to the dog-cart and off they would go to the village. I longed and longed to go with them, and had often suggested as much to Corrie, but she, like me, found it impossible to convey the idea to the family. We understand so much about them, yet they understand so little about us. But I must admit they do try.

Later I saw Puddy and Fionna and Margie set off in the trap, Fionna driving rather cautiously, as she was a learner. Corrie had told me that all her caution was unnecessary, as she would always take care to go properly for Fionna, whether Fionna was riding or driving her. Puddy was a different matter. It sometimes amused Corrie to test Puddy's skill as a horsewoman, and she would play up in a manner which I considered most unladylike. However, I think Puddy enjoyed these arguments quite as much as Corrie did, for she always won in the end. She didn't know that Corrie intended to let her win from the start.

Kitten always slept in the afternoons, and I could

hear Grandpop and John working together at the hen-house. The sound of their hammering must have carried miles across the countryside. Not that it would disturb people, but those who couldn't see what was being made would be wondering who was hammering what, and why. I have already told you that the people here have a great sense of curiosity.

I had several encounters that afternoon, two with field mice and one with a mole, before I caught a fat buck rabbit which I carried with me to one of my favourite eating-places – a sheltered place behind our Standing Stone. This stone is at the top of the drive, near the house. Some say it is a Druid stone, others that it marks the pilgrim way to Iona. And it is also said that treasure lies buried beneath it, but I don't think this can be true, or the family would have been at it with a pick-axe long ago.

I don't wish to boast, but it was clever of me to kill a mole. I wish I could kill more. They play havoc with the fields, and Corrie is afraid of stumbling over the molehills, sure-footed though she is.

I found I could only eat the head and part of one leg of my rabbit, and I wished I had eaten less at breakfast. However, I neatly skinned the shoulders, then hid the remains behind a piece of corrugated iron that was leaning up against the house. Once before, I had left almost a whole rabbit near the house, and Puddy had seen it and taken it and cooked if for Carla, which I considered one of the few unkind things Puddy has ever done to me. I don't think she quite understood that it is no easy task to catch and kill a rabbit as big as oneself. The fact that I often do so is a small matter of prowess, which should not be underestimated.

I was quite surprised to hear the beat of Corrie's hooves trotting back along the road. My hunting must have taken longer than I had realised.

Corrie turned in at the gate and made much of the slight rise in the drive. She gave her low whinny when she saw me, and I heard Fionna say, 'Listen, she's glad to be home.'

Oh dear me! If only I could tell them that it was me she was glad to see.

Margie went into the house with some parcels, and I knew, too, that as it was Tuesday, she'd have bought the postal orders for the football pools. All the family did the pools, and often talked of the wonderful things they would do when they won the seventy-five thousand pounds. I expect almost every cat in Britain has a family that talks the same way. But I'll say for mine that the first thing each of them was going to do was to share it out equally with the others, and, knowing them, it's exactly what they would do. I'd better say now that you mustn't think that this book is going to end with one of them winning the pools and doing all the marvellous things they had planned. Ours is an ordinary family, and I'm not going to introduce anything fancy into this story about them. If you want that sort of thing, you'd better get something else out of your library. Though I must confess it would be just wonderful if it did happen before I reach the end of this story! So there I am, planning to win the pools too – just as silly as the rest of them.

Puddy and Fionna unharnessed Corrie and gave her a quick rub-down with some hay – what they call a whisp. Grandpop and Puddy have long arguments over the question of grooming Corrie. Grandpop says she should be thoroughly groomed daily, as his horses had always been, but Puddy says that his horses lived in stables, whereas Corrie, living out, needs the grass and mud that her coat collects to keep her warm. So Puddy only gives her a light grooming every day, to get rid of the loose hairs of her winter coat, which, now that it was spring, Corrie was shedding.

I asked Corrie which of them was right, and she said both were. A stable-kept horse needs thorough grooming: a horse that lives out requires only a brush-up, though of course the same care must be taken of the feet, whether in the stable or not. So remember that – if you are lucky enough to have a horse of your own. Corrie doesn't wear shoes, as she had particularly hard hooves, but Kaya used to call regularly to pare her hooves and rasp them, and check over her feet.

Kaya, with his round, good-natured face, his wide blue eyes and sturdy Highland figure, was a remarkable person, and one very useful to have in the district, for I think there is nothing he can't do. He helps build houses, mends fences, repairs roads, digs ditches, traps rabbits and even cuts hair. But here we know him best as our blacksmith, and very able he is too. It is a long time since a proper blacksmith worked here – I have already told you that the smithy is falling down – but Puddy says that so long as Kaya is about, she won't worry. And knowing what a worrier Puddy is, I think Kaya must really be good.

Corrie was back in her field now, rewarded with oats. Don't think that Corrie is fed entirely on oats, which would be most unsuitable for her, considering the little work she does. She only gets a handful occasionally, in a bucket, which makes her very happy without making her frisky.

Inside the house, the family were settling down for tea. Kitten had made potato scones, and Fionna's chin was shiny with butter when I arrived at the dining-room window. Fionna is not at all greedy in the ordinary way, but when there are potato scones I notice she eats very fast and has one eye on the plate on which the scones are piled. They don't stay piled for long! All the family love potato scones, but Kitten can't eat them, because if she does she gets indigestion and has to drink hot water and bicarbonate of soda. Bicarbonate of soda is a great medicine with the family, as a gargle, as a poultice or anything else at all. And very good it is too, and cheap.

It was John who noticed me first. 'Oh, Nicky, poor liddle cat!' he said, and came over and opened the window, so that I climbed with dignity onto the big oak chest, studded with brass, which is just below the window, and gives me a good view of the room, at the same time enabling me to keep out of the way of any teasing ideas Carla may have.

The new hen-house was finished, and the question was how to induce the hens to use it. Hens are creatures of habit, and it was going to take some skill to break them of their custom of sleeping where they had always slept. Everyone had different ideas about how to do it, but in the end it was Puddy who went out and caught each one in turn, all ten of them, plus the cock, and dumped them one by one in their new home. I've always thought that hens are the most unintelligent creatures of my acquaintance, and now I know it. They twittered away most indignantly, despite the fact that they now had a huge house with southern aspect, light, airy, and beautifully furnished with perches, laying boxes, a grain hopper and a water trough. It was far, far superior to their old home, and indeed, to any hen-house I have seen. It then occurred to me that my presence at Puddy's feet might have something to do with their fussy protests, so I slipped off back to the house, arriving there just as Johnnie-the-Postman came slowly up the drive, weighed down, as he always was, by his haversack of letters.

Carla was barking as if we were being invaded by burglars. She did this every evening, and anticipated Johnnie's arrival with impatient woofs and whimpers. I never discovered whether, were she let loose, she would eat Johnnie, or fawn over him. I think the family never knew either, for they took good care to hold on to her, so that they would not find out.

Margie met Johnnie halfway up the drive and she gave him the letters the family had written (one was to the fishmonger in Oban ordering fish, one was a postcard to Puddy's library asking for another book and the third was a cheque, sent with much grumbling to John's tailor). He then gave her the letters and papers that had come for them. The *Scotsman*, *The Times*, a begging letter from a charitable organisation, an Account Rendered from John's tailor (which they needn't have bothered to send!) and a buff envelope with OHMS printed in the corner.

Margie glanced at this, then shouted over to the house, 'It's your call-up, I think, John.'

And she was right. But at that time I didn't know what a call-up meant, or how right Corrie had been with her dream.

But I know now.

Chapter Four

Quite suddenly I realised that spring had really come. The daffodils which grow all over the lawns and up the side of the drive had been dreadfully battered by the winds, yet somehow their flamboyance was undefeated, and now, in the light air, they had a look of serene victory. Here and there the narcissi were coming

Margie and John raking hay

into flower, Puddy was cursing the mice that ate the crocuses (and I resolved to redouble my efforts to rid her of these pests) – and the few scanty trees showed signs of bursting into life.

Corrie spent a great deal of her time eating the new, succulent grass that grew at the edge of the bogs in that big wild field where nothing was ever cultivated but which at some time had been used as a peat moss. I was a little afraid that one day Corrie would sink deeply into a bog, but she reassured me, telling me that the special instinct which she had inherited from her moorland ancestors gave her complete security from any mistake that might lead her into trouble.

Earlier that year, John and Puddy had set fire to the heather over that rough field, and I had been saddened to see the blackened wasteland it rapidly became, but I knew that the young heather that would grow up in its place later in the year would be more tender and sweet than the tough heather which had been burned; and green grass was already showing where before there had been no grass visible at all.

One day the family had breakfast earlier than usual, and soon I discovered the reason for this as, with a great roaring of engines, the big tractor, driven by a nearby farmer, came pounding up the drive. Soon the big field was being ploughed, while countless seagulls wheeled overhead and swooped down on the innumerable tit-bits that the over-turned earth revealed.

At about that time, Puddy moved her chickens

from the brooder to an outdoor rearing house. There were seventeen chickens now, as three had died in spite of Puddy's efforts to save them. And what efforts she had made! Each sickly chick was given a cardboard box to itself, and these she spread over the Aga so that Kitten could scarcely cook the meals. For days these chickens were cosseted, and I think it says a lot for the care Puddy took that one of them recovered from whatever ailment it suffered from and was now back with the others, so healthy you couldn't tell which had been the sickly one.

I was interested to see that a family of wild duck had arrived on the loch. They must have lived on one of the islands, but every day they swam around, the parents obviously very proud of their five ducklings. There were swans on the loch too. Six of them, and very handsome they were, but I knew they would not make their permanent home there. Autumn and spring, they arrive on their way somewhere else, but where they come from and where they go to, I have never discovered. It was the same with the wild geese, who came and went and never stayed.

When the ploughing was finished, the big field was harrowed, and after that, there was a lot of work for John and Puddy and Fionna to do, spreading lime and manure, and planting seeds. First of all, John got out Puffing Billy, which is the name of the little tractor belonging to the family, and he loaded Puffing Billy's trailer with sacks of lime, and chugged round the field, dropping off sacks at regular intervals. Fionna and

Puddy undid the sacks and scattered the lime with a spade, and I've never seen such a sight as they were when they had finished! They looked as if they had been rolled in flour, and although I kept my distance during these operations, I found that even I had collected a good deal of the horrid white stuff, carried over in the wind.

After the lime, the artificial manure was spread, and this was gritty stuff, so it didn't blow about so much. Then the seed was sown, and Puddy, John and Fionna must have walked miles, up and down the field, scattering the oats, which they carried in a specially constructed sack-cloth container slung round their necks. Corrie was very good about the oats. She would lean over the railing which divided the big field from the wild field where she now lived, and her nostrils would quiver with excitement, but she made no attempt to crash her way through the fencing. And I know she could do that easily enough if she tried!

When the planting was finished, every day Fionna peered round the field to see if the shoots were showing, and one day John managed to shoot one of the hoody crows that guzzle the seeds and are a menace to farmers and crofters in these parts. He hung up the dead crow on a pole in the middle of the field, and for a long time the crows stayed away. Crows always avoid, for a while, the place where one of them has been killed.

One day Margie and John and Puddy and Fionna set off in Florrie, which is the little black Ford with yellow wheels, and I knew that they were going to the displenishing sale of one of the big houses at the other end of the island, for I've heard them talk about it. I didn't know what a displenishing sale was when they left, but my word, I knew when they came back! There was hardly room for them to sit in Florrie, so piled up she was with cake-tins, rusty paraffin stoves, odd pieces of crockery and nameless objects, one of which was a water softener, bought by John for a shilling. He was very pleased with this, though it turned out to be broken and quite useless.

Grandpop had some grumbles about bringing all this rubbish home, but when a wee while later a lorry arrived with a heap of furniture as well, he was speechless! However, Margie pointed out that Victorian chests of drawers were useful, and so are chaff-cutters and spinning-wheels, and the huge dresser was the very thing for the kitchen.

Somehow or other, most of the things were fitted into the house, though it meant quite a lot of other things had to be shifted out to the cottage. And in next to no time the family were wondering how they had ever managed without the tall-boy in the cloakroom or the huge dresser in the kitchen. Which just goes to show that things do come in useful, if you have a mind that they shall.

Another excitement was the Ploughing Match. This is held every year, and the new-fangled tractors are put aside and replaced by the horse, which I am sure you will agree is a far better means of drawing a plough, for a horse does not stick in the mud or get fuel trouble. And my word! how grand the competing horses looked as they arrived proudly at the field where the match was to take place!

I had arrived at the scene early, for I realised that the family would never think of taking me with them in Florrie, and I found that my cross-country walk had taken less time than I had expected. I therefore sat at the gate of the competition field and watched the horses arriving, in pairs, their harness polished till it shone, their manes and tails plaited and tied up with coloured ribbon. Indeed, so splendid did each pair look that at first I did not recognise Sandy and Queenie, the two smart cart-horses who so often passed our house and talked to Corrie over the wall.

I settled myself in a quiet place among some rushes, for the wind was bitterly cold, and there I watched it all – the arrival of my family, laughing and chatting, and slapping at Carla when she tried to get too friendly with other dogs, the patient horses obeying the crisp instructions of their drivers, the black, peaty soil turned back in neat furrows, the seagulls sweeping and crying in their wake.

Watching them, men and horses working together, I wondered why Man has allowed his desire for speed to displace his most generous helpmate, the horse. And I confess that my heart was filled with sadness to think of the faithful horses who had gone to the knackers so that brightly painted tractors might occupy their stalls. And at the end of the day, with that perfectly ploughed field spread before them, and with their horses – many of whom now wore a prize rosette fixed to their bridles – wending a weary but resolute way home, I hoped the farmers shared my sentiments and would resolve that they at least would give the horse the place in the community which he deserves.

Most days there weren't displenishing sales or ploughing matches to go to, and then Puddy and Fionna would go out with Corrie, either in the dog-cart or for a ride, but in spite of this, Corrie was getting very fat on the new spring grass. The goats too were thriving on the new growth, though their preference was for nettles and the new shoots of whin, and their milk had increased so much that Kitten made butter every few days, shaking up the cream in a glass jar. Puddy was also able to give goat's milk to a sick farmer, and if you suffer from a bad digestion, I can tell you that goat's milk is the very thing for you. And don't say you don't like it, for pure, clean goat's milk has no more taste or smell than clean cow's milk. It needs the addition of a little sugar, as it is not very sweet, but if you have the idea that it is strong-tasting and smelly, you are absolutely wrong.

One day Puddy set off on Corrie, with her can of goat's milk for the sick farmer, and she had hardly started when somehow or other she managed to fall off Corrie's wide back and landed flat on her back in the heather. But amazingly she kept the can upright and never spilt a drop of milk! I was sitting on the wall and saw it happen, and I must admit it was quite enough to make a human laugh! Corrie of course stood quite still as soon as she felt Puddy disappear. Even if she had been galloping – and she was only trotting – she would have stood still, for that is the nature of Highland ponies, and very useful it is too, if you are nervous or learning to ride. I noticed that after this episode, Puddy delivered the milk on Fionna's bicycle. This wasn't because she'd been hurt, because you can't get hurt falling on a clump of heather, but perhaps she had noticed me on the wall and felt she must not risk looking so foolish in front of me again.

I have said that Corrie and the goats were flourishing, so it is only fair to mention that I, too, was putting on a considerable amount of weight. Young rabbits are very tasty, and comparatively easy to catch, and if at times I ate rather more than was good for my figure, well, you can hardly blame me. Besides, at this time of year there were a few rather attractive young tabbies that I had my eye on, and even though, without wishing to be thought conceited, I knew I was the best catch in the south of Mull, I knew too that there would be certain toms who would be anxious to contest me. So I needed my strength for my romantic future, with long distances to travel and with a fight to face before victorious return.

In the house a great deal of packing was going on. Fionna's trunk was being got ready for her return to school, and this meant checking through long lists of clothing which she had to take back with her, while Puddy and Kitten, and indeed all the family, grumbled about the petty regulations which schools impose upon one. Fionna had little to do with this preparation of her possessions, preferring to cycle round the country, armed with a pencil and notebook in which she recorded the habits of birds. This is a veritable paradise for a birdwatcher, and I should know, for I've done long hours of it myself, though not with the intention of recording my observations. And if you think that my thoughts were focused on the tasty meal this or that bird might provide, you are not far wrong, though I've said it before and I say it again – the family love the birds so I leave them alone. I'm an affectionate cat and I like to please.

It was not only Fionna who was packing. Margie was so much better now that she was going back to London, and she would soon be working again at the film studio near the pet-shop where first I met my family. I often climbed on her knee and rubbed myself against her and tried to make her understand that there were messages I wanted to send to my old friends in Ealing. But it was no good. She tickled my ears and said endearing things to me, but of the things I was telling her she had no idea. So I gave up and went to see Corrie, to tell her more stories about London, of which she never tired.

Corrie had a great ambition to visit London, and her dream was that one day she would take part in the Horse of the Year Show, and would parade in the very same arena that rang with applause for Foxhunter and Tosca and Winston-the-Horse-the-Queen-rides. But in Corrie's dream, the chief applause would be for Corrieshellach, and the band would play 'The Road to the Isles' as she marched proudly under the spotlight, her silver mane flowing and her silver tail skimming the ground with almost nothing to spare. For it would be Corrie's beauty that would win her a place in that parade, and beauty in a Highland pony means that very long, flowing tail and other virtues besides. All of which Corrie possess a hundredfold.

The third lot of packing was being done by John, whenever he wasn't digging ditches or repairing fences or doing his Russian dance and asking for FOOD. John's packing meant digging through luggage in an outhouse, and scattering all manner of strange objects around the backyard. There were long black tin trunks, which he called his uniform cases, and there was a canvas hold-all for bedding, and a camp basin and a mosquito whisk. This latter he said he wouldn't need in Stirling.

Crumpled khaki uniform was brought out of the cases, and the anti-moth powder shaken out. Then Kitten hung the things in the sun and dared the goats to eat them. The tunic of the suit had several coloured ribbons on the left breast and three gold stripes on the right arm, which Puddy said were 'wound stripes'. This meant that John had been through a very bad time during the war. I would like to have told them that there would not be room on my coat for all my wound stripes, but perhaps they would have thought me frivolous.

John had left the army after the war and had gone back to Oxford University. After that, he had written a lot of film scripts, which kept him travelling round the world, but soon he decided he would rather be in the army and had given up films. He had come home to Mull, waiting for his call-up. And that was the OHMS envelope I told you about in my last chapter.

Corrie watched these preparations sadly. She didn't say, 'It's chust like I told you.' She would consider that boastful, and Corrie is the most self-effacing mare I have ever met. But she knew, as I did, that when John left, it would not be in the bus, and that his going would be for a much longer time than Margie's or Fionna's would be. Even the goats must have had a sense of impending loss, for they chewed the cud much more thoughtfully than ever before, and sometimes I noticed that there was a tear in Flora's eye. (I have since discovered I was wrong about that. Puddy cured Flora's tears with boracic eye-lotion.)

But before John left, a very big and important and sad thing was to happen. So big and so important that, although, like I said, it has now become just a point of time, when the family say, 'That was before the foot and mouth' or 'That was after the foot and mouth,' it still sends a chill down my spine.

Yes, that tells you what happened. No sooner had Fionna and Margie gone, leaving a very empty feeling of sadness behind them, than the shocking news spread like magic through the district. Foot and mouth disease had struck the Isle of Mull. Cattle only two miles away were infected. Eight vets were already on their way to supervise the slaughter of contacts. Yes, SLAUGHTER. I've written it huge because that's what it was. HUGE.

And these memories have so upset me that I'll have to stop writing about them until tomorrow.

CHAPTER FIVE

There was a bath of disinfectant at the front gate. There was a bath of disinfectant at the side gate. There was a bath of disinfectant at the back gate. And anyone entering our grounds had to wash his shoes in that disinfectant before entering the gates. Rushes soaked in disinfectant were spread on the drive, to clean the wheels of any approaching cars, and every day a vet

Arnish butting Flora

called to look at the goats and the bullocks. These vets wore gumboots and mackintoshes and sou'westers so that they could be sprayed with disinfectant before and after their visits. This must have been very trying, for the weather was warm and it was necessary for them to walk many miles every day on their tours of inspection, because their cars could not get by road to anything like all the suspect crofts and farms.

Let me say here and now that nobody could have carried out a hateful, indeed repugnant, job more tactfully and with greater thoughtfulness than did those vets. Every cloven-hooved beast in a given area had to be destroyed. That was the law and it had to be carried out, no matter what private opinions there might have been about this wholesale slaughter. But the distress this edict wrought can scarcely be described.

Often and often the family had grumbled at the stray flocks of sheep which had a way of finding our land more tasty than the vast areas they were supposed to graze, and consequently it was very difficult to keep them from climbing into our fields, knocking down the stones from the top of the walls and doing no end of minor damage. Now it was known that these very sheep would have to be destroyed, the family would gladly knock down the walls themselves to admit the poor victims, if by doing so, they could have given them sanctuary. But of course that couldn't be.

No time was wasted in carrying out the slaughter policy. A huge pit was dug in the waste land behind our house, and on a bright Saturday in May the macabre procession of cattle moved along the road to the pit. There was a shot, a flick of a tail, and the animal fell into the pit, to be followed by the next animal. Finally, the calves were led to the pit, and those too small to walk were carried.

Afterwards a lorry laden with quicklime was driven up to the pit, and a crowd of men got busy with spades, first shovelling in the quicklime, then covering up the huge grave. And that was that. I don't know where the sheep were buried, lambs and all, and I never enquired.

I've told you as briefly as possible, because I don't want to disgust you or tear at your heartstrings. But I expect when you hear about outbreaks of foot and mouth on the wireless, you think all the important news is over, so you just switch off and never give it another thought. Unless it is in your area and the animals that have been part of the landscape are suddenly there no more, and the people you know, who have reared and loved those animals, are faced with this terrible loss; then you realise what that brief announcement means, and you pause to think and pity and wish you could help.

By great good fortune, the area to be cleared for the present outbreak ended at the side road over by the church. That meant there was some waste ground between us and the infected land. At any moment an animal on our side of the road might become infected, and that would mean our own bullocks and goats would have to go to a horrid pit somewhere.

I think Puddy's worryings must have been beyond

imagining, for she worried so much anyhow! She tethered Arnish and Flora so that they could not leave our grounds; she reinforced the fence, so that there was no chance of the bullocks escaping, and she would not take Corrie out on the road for fear of carrying home germs. Corrie became quite incredibly fat – but that is to digress.

When Carla was taken for walks, she was dipped in the tub of disinfectant on her return home, and from that time to this, Carla hates walks, remembering always that horrid ducking.

In order to help, I gave up my courtship of a particularly attractive young cat at Kintra (one of the villages in the infected area) and confined my activities to wiping out a few more rabbits and a great many mice. But a little incident will show you how thoughtless one can be – even I, who pride myself in trying to please.

Just after the foot and mouth outbreak, when the vets had first arrived and everyone was feeling rather confused, I set off for Kintra, and because of a contretemps with a couple of rivals, I stayed there rather longer than I had expected. A couple of days in fact. Returning home one afternoon and feeling, I may say, rather the worse for wear, I found Puddy at the front gate, talking to two of the vets.

'We have absolutely no contacts with anything outside our own land,' I could hear her saying. 'I never even take the pony out. So you can't think that the goats are likely to be infected. Nothing from here goes anywhere else.'

Imagine how I felt as I approached the gate! It was too late to slip away and hide, for already I had been seen. I could feel Puddy looking at me in dismay and anxiety, and I knew the vets were looking at me too. She went on talking to distract their attention. I climbed under the gate, and very carefully and deliberately walked in a circle round the disinfected straw. It was the best I could do, to undo the wrong I had done, though I hated the smell of the disinfectant, and knew that I would hate still more licking it off my paws. It might even kill me, but if I had brought germs to my dear friends, I deserved to die.

I was so ashamed that I scarcely went near the house for days, except for meals. I lived in daily dread that one of our animals would break out with the disease. I told Corrie something of my fears, but not everything, for I did not want to distress her kindly heart too deeply. She was already much upset, for all round us the still, quiet countryside seemed to impress on us, in its strange silence, the catastrophe that had befallen our land.

Then one day, with my anxiety almost at breaking point, Puddy came out and untethered the goats. 'We're out of quarantine. We're safe,' she told them delightedly, and Arnish rose up on her hind legs and dived down on Flora, just for the sheer joy of being released from captivity. Whether she knew the reason for that tether, I have no idea, but I overheard her saying to Flora that this was the result of having Tories in power. It was a shocking statement, but I had long ago found that politically-minded people don't care at all what outrageous and untrue statements they make about one another, so it's no use getting upset about it. However, I resolved that I would avoid politics, and so avoid having to tell a pack of lies to my friends.

It would be a while before the people whose animals had been destroyed would be allowed to re-stock, so the air of sadness hung over the district for some time. Those few who, like us, had escaped, talked in hushed voices of their good fortune, and of their sympathy for the ones who suffered.

The disinfectant tubs were removed from the gates (the straw had blown away from the drive long ago) – and the urgent notices warning people about infected property were removed. Corrie was taken out on the road and sweated so much with the little scrap of exercise that Puddy had a fit of worrying about her, fearing she might get pneumonia. Carla continued to slink away, avoiding walks. Peter and Iain chewed the cud and appeared not to know anything had ever been amiss, and Arnish redoubled her propaganda about the New Era.

Inside the house, Kitten cooked and cleaned, and Grandpop mended things – the car, the roof, the electric-lighting plant, anything that was broken at all. And as he mended, he hummed his little hums, partic-ularly one about counting your blessings, which he had heard sung during Community Hymn Singing on the wireless, and which reminded him of his happy student days in Edinburgh – days which he never ceased to recall and which made him sometimes feel very nostalgic. John finished his packing and his fencing and his instructions to Puddy about what she was to do while he was away. Then one day he and all his baggage were heaped into Florrie, and Puddy drove him off, and returned much later, alone.

So he left in the car, not the bus, which showed that his departure was important. As the car left the drive, Corrie neighed and I meowed, but I'm afraid he never heard us.

There is something wrong with Florrie's silencer, and a little meow and a low whinny could never penetrate through the din of the engine. All the same, we did our best, and some day, if he reads these words, he'll know we are thinking of him and loving him yet.

CHAPTER SIX

Puddy is not the sort to sit down under depression and mope. On the day that horrid pit was dug, she moved a broody hen into a box and she went off in Florrie to a farm right out of earshot of the sound of the humane killer, and she brought back twelve duck eggs, which she set under the broody hen. After that, she was in a constant state of worry about the rats eating the eggs, and you'd never believe the number of contraptions she erected round that box to keep it rat-proof.

Ducks

Then one day Archie-the-Carrier arrived with his lorry, and on the lorry he had a beautiful rat-proof coop and run that Puddy had ordered from the mainland. Very carefully she transferred the hen and the eggs into their new home, and after that she didn't worry about rats any more.

Archie-the-Carrier paid us lots of visits, as he brought the sacks of grain, the manure, the fencing stobs, wire netting and indeed every manner of thing that could not be bought in the village store. Archie was always very cheerful and in windy weather he kept his hat tied on with string. Whenever the family thanked him for bringing things he said, 'You're welcome,' which I think is one of the nicest ways of telling people that you are happy to serve them.

The oats were showing very green now, and Puddy was working busily in the garden, a very unrewarding task, for the rabbits somehow always managed to find a way in, and they made havoc with the things she tried to grow. She now chose flowers that they didn't like eating, such as gladioli and lupins, but unfortunately she couldn't do the same with vegetables. The fruit trees she had planted last year were in blossom but I feared the wind would blacken the leaves before the fruit began to form. I was wrong here, for two of the trees produced quite good red apples which Kitten picked before the wind could blow them off. Before John left, he planted four poplar trees as an experiment. There is a high hawthorn hedge round the west and north sides of the garden, but it does not give enough protection from the wind, and if these poplars are a success Puddy means to plant more, just inside the hawthorns. On the east side there is fencing, and laburnum and lilac trees. The laburnum flowered beautifully but the lilac never seems to flower. On the south there is a privet hedge, which divides the garden from part of the paddock. Corrie once came through this hedge to have a look at the garden, so now it is reinforced with a low wall.

Mostly the garden grows weeds, and when I say weeds, I don't mean the odd dandelion. Puddy's weeds are champions, the burrs being perhaps the biggest and the best, with leaves the size of a tennis racquet, and they tower over Puddy, who says the roots are twice the length of her height.

The cuckoo had arrived, and we were never allowed to forget it for long. The skylarks, who build their nests on the ground – the wild field where Corrie now lives was a favourite spot – flung their glorious song as they flew higher and higher, vanishing like a speck into the sky, and I believe that even if the family didn't love birds, I would never touch a skylark, even though many's the time I've almost trodden on their nests. Perhaps I must be a musical cat, for I always notice the song of birds. And you should hear the blackbirds, who like to perch on the chimney stacks and give a recital to warm the cockles of your heart. But if you know what the cockles of your heart are, you are cleverer than I am.

Kitten was wonderful with birds. She would stand at the back door, throwing crumbs and whistling, and in no time she would have birds of all sorts hopping round her, quite unafraid. Then the goats would come clicking along to join the party, and off would fly the birds, to Kitten's annoyance, and the goats' pleasure. This was very tiresome of the goats, for normally they will not touch any tit-bit that falls on the ground.

Johnnie-the-Postman was always very much looked forward to, as I've told you already, but now, with only half the family at home, the arrival of the mail was more important than ever. Fionna's letter came once a week, on Monday unless for some reason it had missed the collection, and when this happened it came on Tuesday. Fionna's letters were brief, rather messy and absolutely full of drawings, mostly of horses. During the autumn term, she gave the score of the hockey matches which her boarding house played against other houses; in spring she gave the score of the lacrosse matches and in the summer the cricket and tennis matches. And she wrote about Gilly and Jelly and Horsey and Sago, but they were nothing to do with food, as you might suppose. They were the names of her friends, and for a time I wondered what their godfathers and godmothers must have been thinking about, giving the children such names. Then I realised that they were probably pet-names, like Puddy and Kitten, so perhaps their godfathers and godmothers weren't so thoughtless after all.

Margie's letters came every few days, written very big so that they looked very long until you read them. Margie was absolutely well now and wished she could leave London and live in Mull for ever. John's letters were long when they came, which wasn't often. They were always very cheerful, and Puddy said that even when he was snowed up in the trenches in Italy during the war, his letters had been cheerful. So as he was living in Stirling Castle, I suppose he could feel very cheery indeed. Secretly I was most impressed by his address – Stirling Castle. I made a point of reading about it in the history books in the cottage, and exciting reading it made too. The names it conjured up – the Black Douglas, Robert the Bruce and Mary, Queen of Scots. After a while I became a fervent Scottish Nationalist until I remembered the dire effects being political had on people, and not wanting to become narrow-minded like Arnish, I read the Elizabethan voyages of discovery and my sense of balance was restored.

Just four weeks after Puddy had put the eggs under the broody hen, she came into the house very flushed and excited, saying that she could hear cheeping under the hen and could just see one egg half open and a feathery duckling inside. I made an excuse to go out of doors, for I wanted to see the miracle myself. However, the hen looked so angry when she saw me approach, and she fluffed her feathers so indignantly, that I pretended I was simply walking past and stalked off into the garden. Don't think I was afraid of that hen – not me! Besides, the wire netting that kept the rats out of the run also kept the hen inside. But I had heard that hens at this time are in an odd mental condition, and may kill the chicks if danger threatens. That hen should know by now that I'm not Danger; all the same, it wouldn't do to run risks, and I just don't know what Puddy would do if she lost her ducklings now, just as they were hatching.

The next morning, Puddy was down early, and I left the electric-lighting plant house, where I had spent the night, as soon as I heard her open the kitchen door. Carla greeted me with more exuberance than seemed to me necessary, and when I had righted myself from the somersault I had unwittingly turned, I followed Puddy to the coop, and there, sure enough, was the broody hen and eight tiny ducklings with golden bills and huge web feet! Carla and I sat quietly together, for Carla can be quiet if she likes, while Puddy removed the four eggs that had not hatched, together with the empty egg-shells. Then she put some clean straw gently under the hen, and added a dish of water alongside the food she had already placed in the run. The ducklings scuttled quickly under their foster-mother but soon they were out again, splashing in the water. It's a curious fact that while a new-born duckling enjoys a swim, it will die of chill if caught in the rain. I wondered if Puddy knew this, and soon found that she did, for whenever there was a drop of rain, she covered that coop with a tarpaulin. And this she did till the ducklings, who grew at an astonishing rate, were quite able to withstand all manner of weather.

That poor hen must have wondered a lot about the curious shape her chicks had become. I often saw her look at the other baby chicks, who were now running around in the hen-run, and when she could, she pecked at them through the bars. I put this down to jealousy. She must have resented those chicks looking so much prettier, as she thought, than her own brood. Personally, I found the ducklings enchanting, with their khaki feathers and yellow chests. Later on, two of them developed bright bills and more vivid feathers, and those, Puddy said, were the drakes and would be the first for the pot. Which I considered was most unfeeling of her.

I heard Puddy say to Grandpop and Kitten that the hatching of those eggs quite made up for the dreadful slaughter of the animals, and I could understand what she meant. In the balance of things, eight little ducks don't add up to much compared with hundreds of head of cattle, yet the very fact that an apparently dead thing like an egg can turn into a living thing like a duckling is a startling and wonderful manifestation, if you think of it at all. That's why I called it a miracle when I first referred to it. People wouldn't want to have seas dividing and rivers running backwards if they'd stop to think seriously about eggs.

This brings me to a personal matter, which in fact my dissertation on eggs is leading up to. I had become the father of five lively kittens, three girls and two boys. Their mother was a wild cat with whom I had become friendly, and she had a nice home for them in a rabbit-hole under a whin bush in Corrie's wild field. Don't think that when I say the mother was a wild cat I mean one of the big snarling brutes still to be found in remote parts of Scotland. The wild cats in Mull are descendants of domestic cats, probably some of those left behind at the time of the dispersal of the Highlanders.

At Carsaig in Mull there is a herd of wild goats that can be traced back to that dreadful time. I'm not going to give you the history of the Clearances, because it makes me so angry that I get political, which I don't want to be. But I can tell you that many good Highlanders were turned out of their homes and shipped off to Canada and other places so that their land could be used for deer-stalking, a pastime of rich people from far away. Puddy's grandmother used to tell Puddy of the ships laden with weeping people being sent away to unknown shores. Puddy's grandmother had seen it herself when she was a young girl, and that is the nearest I can get to an eyewitness account, for it happened over a hundred years ago.

In case I have depressed you, I'll just add that the descendants of many of those people are rich men today in the New World. I'm not excusing what happened when I tell you this, but there it is.

One day I was sitting on the wall by the gate, worrying a little I confess, as during the past few days I had become the father of three more families, which I think you will agree, is too much of a good thing. Puddy was weeding the drive. That is to say, she was spraying it with a special preparation made out of water and sodium chlorate. This is death to weeds and harmless to animals, so it was just the thing for us, and for you, too, if you have weeds and animals as we have.

I saw Kaya coming along the road before Puddy saw him. Kaya had bunches of rabbits dangling from each side of the handlebars of his bicycle. He was pushing the bicycle, so perhaps he had a puncture. When he reached the gate, he had to stop and watch Puddy and ask her what she was doing. She explained about sodium chlorate and animals, and he said that was just grand. At this point my attention was distracted by a fly, and when I had disposed of it, I was shocked to hear Puddy saying, 'I've arranged for her to travel by the cattle boat from Bunessan, then she'll go by train to Perth. But I don't want to take her to the boat myself. I'd so hate saying goodbye.'

'Chust you give me her halter and I'll see to it all for you,' Kaya said comfortably. 'And it's good luck I'll wish her, I'm sure.'

They talked some more, but I was too heartsick to hear what they said. Puddy was sending Corrie away! I had to repeat it over and over to get the sense of it. It couldn't be true. She loved Corrie. But why else would Corrie be sent to a boat, and then by train to Perth?

My family affairs had kept me out of the house for some days, so I had heard no murmur of this impending disaster.

I slunk up the drive and found Carla lying in the grass, not far from Puddy of course. I sat beside her, and seeing that she was in a quiet mood, I poured out my troubles to her. I had to tell somebody, and I could not tell Corrie of her fate.

Carla was very nice. I've forgiven her for all the bouncings she's given me before and since, because she was so kind when I needed comfort so badly.

'I'm always with the family, I hear every word they say,' she said. This was true, though I wondered whether her volatile mind took in what happened around her. 'And' – she paused, to give her words impact – 'I can put your mind absolutely at ease. CORRIE IS GOING TO A SHOW.'

'A show?' I sat bolt upright, in dismay.

'Yes, the family think her beauty is wasted here. So they've had a whip-round and they're sending her to Perth, where she came from, to get groomed. Then she's going to a show.' She snapped at a fly, then rolled over on her back. This meant she wanted to play, and already her interest was wandering.

'What show is she going to?' I asked quickly.

'The best of course. The Royal Highland.' She sat up abruptly as Puddy disappeared outside the gate. In a moment she had scampered off too, though she knew as well as I did that Puddy was only seeing Kaya off, and wouldn't go far.

The Royal Highland Show! Oh the relief I felt, and the joy. Corrie was going to the Royal Highland, and of course she would win the first prize and come home in a blaze of glory! And maybe her dream would come true, and she'd be invited to the big show in London.

I set off to tell her. Then I paused for thought. Either she knew about it and didn't want to tell me yet, knowing how much I would miss her. Or she didn't know, and I must let Puddy be the one to tell her.

And with great self-control, I retraced my steps and returned to the wall.

CHAPTER SEVEN

It was not long before everyone in the neighbourhood was talking about Corrieshellach and the Highland Show. There was such pride and such excitement that you'd think she belonged to them all, and not just to the family.

Corrie took being a celebrity very calmly, indeed she protested at my calling her a celebrity at all. 'Och,

Kitten and Nicky in the garden

maybe I'll chust be thrown out of the ring with the rubbish,' she said, 'and I'll make a fool of myself after all.'

Several times a week now a bus would pass our gates, taking people on a tour between Tobermory and Iona. The bus of course didn't cross to Iona, for there is no car ferry, but the people got off at Fionnphort, and Angus or Dan, the two ferrymen, would be waiting there with the smart white motor boat to take them across the mile or so of sea. There are wonderful things to see in Iona, and if you've never been, you'd better start saving up to go right now. You'll wonder at me telling you that, for I've already remarked that I don't know why people go there instead of staying on lovely Mull. Well, I've learnt what the attraction is, and I hope you'll realise how ready I am to admit when I've been wrong about something.

If I were to tell you all about Iona, I would have to plunge back through the centuries, right to the year when St Columba, with his band of monks, arrived from Ireland and set about converting the Druids, bringing that religion called Christianity to western Scotland. I doubt if I would finish that history before my dying day, even with all the lives I'm supposed to possess. So I'll have to leave all that to the historians, for they have longer lives than cats, and instead I'll just say that St Columba founded an abbey in Iona, and later a nunnery was built, and although through the ages both of these had fallen to ruin, and had been rebuilt and altered, there came a time when they were ruins again. At last money was raised and the abbey restored, but all the surrounding buildings remained little more than a heap of stones. And so it might have been for ever, had not a very good minister devised a scheme for rebuilding the abbey precincts, and at the same time remoulding the lives of the people who built it.

All sorts of people there are; ministers, labourers, rich men from big estates, poor men from the cities. Every summer they come, and they all share in the work of rebuilding, and though they haven't finished yet, there is not much more to do. Meanwhile, they live cheerfully and helpfully on the island, and in the winter they return to their normal work. Usually this is helping to bring the joy of Iona into the depth of the slums, and of course they carry on the work started by St Columba by preaching Christianity to the people who perhaps hadn't much bothered about it before.

I might not have heard any of this myself had not John become interested in the work, and it wasn't long before being interested compelled him to take an active part. He would spend days on end in Iona, busy digging up stones, cutting grass, pushing wheel-barrows, singing in the choir; and when he came back home he would talk of what he had been doing, and I too became infected with his enthusiasm. So one day I slipped into the ferry boat and I went over to see for myself. Now when the buses pass our gate I envy the people inside them, and I hope they will be as impressed with Iona as I was.

I hope you will not think it improper for me to touch upon a religious subject. I don't think you will, as people who think like that wouldn't read this book. Remember the ox and the ass in the stable in Bethlehem? It's a pity the narrator didn't mention the stable cat, but of course with such a terrific thing to write about, he couldn't recount everything. There are people who forget that animals also are the work of the Creator, but since Corrie told me about Horseman's Sunday, I have taken heart, for it shows that there are plenty people too who understand.

One day the bus stopped near our gate on its way back to Tobermory, and I saw the people inside peer through the windows, and I saw the driver's arm pointing over to Corrie, who was unselfconsciously munching in the field beside the loch. I sidled up to the bus, and I heard what I knew I would hear. The driver was telling the people about Corrieshellach going to the show. I was proud! And when the bus moved on, I went down to tell Corrie. But before I could speak, she had something to tell me.

'When I am away,' she said, 'I am going to be put to a very fine stallion, the champion at last year's show. And then I'll have a foal.'

A foal! I was too excited to speak, but I knew Corrie would understand my silence. With the blue sky above, and the loch lapping in gentle froth against the red sand surrounding it, and Corrie's soft munching nearness, this must be the happiest time of my life. And here I think I was right, for it was not many days later that Kaya came, and Puddy gave him the halter, and Corrie, who usually came the moment she saw the halter, was suddenly afraid of the journey, and strangers, and all the unknown terrors of a show, so that she dodged away just before the halter was slipped over her head. Even the bucket of oats failed to tempt her, but when finally she was caught she submitted with that grace that is an enchanting part of her character, and clumped off along the road, evidently resolved that she would give Kaya no further trouble on their five-mile trek to the boat.

I watched her go. I watched until she had disappeared round the little hillock, a mile up the road. Then I returned sadly to the house, where I found Kitten and Grandpop and Puddy, who had been watching Corrie's departure from a window, and were now talking very hard to impress on each other that nothing special had happened, and preparing that beverage which humans find so comforting when things aren't right. Tea.

Carla was there too, of course, nonchalantly chewing at her rubber bone. How she can chew and chew at that bone is beyond me. She must have discovered long ago that it conceals no tasty morsel inside. It's not as if she were teething.

Time never stands still. Doesn't that sound profound, until you pause and realise what a silly obvious thing it is to write! However, I've noticed that most of the profound books I've read are full of mundane facts, wrapped up to sound grandiose and clever. So I'll not delete it, as I ought.

Kitten began preparing Fionna's bedroom. When any of the family were away, you knew weeks before they returned that they were coming back because Kitten got busy airing the bedding and polishing the furniture, and airing the bedding all over again. This was because she was so excited that making preparations seemed to hasten the day of arrival.

On the day itself, Puddy would be up earlier than ever to get the morning tea, which she would carry up to Kitten and Grandpop on a tray, and they'd have a good grumble about the cost of living. At least, from the odd snatches of conversation I've caught, that's what I think they talked about.

After breakfast the house had a bigger cleaning than usual, so I don't know how the carpets stood the wear and tear. Then Kitten went into the garden and picked some of the flowers that had managed to survive the wind and the rain and the rabbits and Puddy's church decorations. When she had finished arranging them, the house looked lovely, and the little pink vase on Fionna's blue dressing table was just right for the rosebuds Kitten had put in it.

Then I got a surprise. I had been so busy watching the bed airing in Fionna's room that I hadn't noticed that Kitten had been carrying out the same rite in Margie's room. If I had been sensible, I would have realised someone must be travelling with Fionna, who could only go under school escort as far as Glasgow. Kitten or Grandpop or Puddy used to meet her there, which meant leaving Mull the day before she was due to arrive. And as they were all here, and none of them over meeting her, then Margie must be coming on holiday too.

Florrie was in disgrace, as she had developed a tiresome habit of stopping, due to a petrol block. A moment's tinkering with her engine and off she'd go again, but getting out and tinkering with her every few miles was a nuisance, so she was not taken on long outings until the man from the garage in Oban could come over and sort her. The trouble about cars is that, being inanimate objects, you can't appeal to their better selves.

It was therefore by bus that Margie and Fionna came, and I sat in the window of Grandpop's study, which had a good view of the road, right to where it disappeared around the hillock. When we saw the white top of the bus, Grandpop called out, 'Here they come!' and Puddy and Carla ran helter skelter down to the gate, while Kitten and Grandpop followed more slowly, Grandpop humming his little hum.

Because of the twisty road, they were all at the gate before the bus. As a matter of fact, it had stopped at the cross road by the old smithy to let someone off, but I was the only one who noticed that. When it arrived Fionna was first to fling herself out, hugging and kissing everyone, while Margie and Neilachan (you remember, he's the driver) dived about among the mailbags stored in the back compartment of the bus, and hauled out their cases. Fionna's trunk wasn't there, as Archie would bring it on his lorry on Thursday.

There were a lot of people on the bus, and it was the big bus too. Sometimes at this time of year there were as many as four buses, one being the HUGE bus. But the family never travelled in that. Nearly all the people on the bus were visitors to Iona. Some of them looked rather sick after the long, bumpy drive.

I had kept a little distance away during all the greetings, as excitement would make Carla very bouncy. But both Fionna and Margie noticed me and stooped down to pet me. When we all went up the drive, we found Arnish and Flora peering through the big white gate that keeps them from getting to the front of the house. Sometimes somebody forgets and leaves the gate open, and in no time Flora and Arnish are through, eating the rambler roses and ivy which for years and years the family have tried to grow against the house.

Fionna and Margie stopped to greet them, too, and by the time they went into the house Kitten and Puddy had put the big willow-pattern teapot on the table in the dining-room, and had dished out the bacon and eggs. It was a family tradition that high tea was served whenever anyone arrived home, and the high tea was all that one could dream about. There were plates of pancakes and scones and potato scones and ginger cake and a fruit cake – and an iced cake with 'Welcome Home' written on it in chocolate. Kitten had been very busy cooking as well as airing beds.

After tea the cases were unpacked and of course Margie had presents for everyone. She had also brought a present for me, a nice packet of 'Katteo'. To tell the truth, I don't much care for 'Katteo', preferring the 'Lassie' Margie had brought for Carla. But I'd eat it with relish, so's not to hurt her feelings. Please note, I have deliberately given an invented name to that cat food. This is so that I can't be sued.

Margie and Fionna spent the evening looking round at the changes which had happened in their absence. Puddy's chickens were now white hens; the ducklings were so big they looked like ducks; Peter and Iain were quite tame, and didn't mind being stroked; the grass in the paddock had turned into hay; and the oats were tall and beginning to turn gold. The heather and bog myrtle, growing profusely all over the moorland, gave the air that delicious scent which, mingled with the smell of seaweed, is the 'Tangle of the Isles' that poets write about. Flora and Arnish staged a boxing match to show how pleased they were to have more of the family home, and I felt very content with life, except for one thing.

There was still a background sadness in my mind, because of a very big disappointment I had recently suffered. I have put off writing about it because I just didn't want to see it in print. Yes, I think you've guessed it. Corrieshellach didn't win the first prize at the show. It's true she won the third prize, and her name was in all the papers, and people rang up and congratulated Puddy and said that in the biggest show in Scotland, third prize was very, very good indeed. I've no doubt it is, but I've no doubt either that Corrie is the most beautiful mare in Britain, and people should know that as well as I do. I'm not saying the judging wasn't fair. Don't think that. But I say the judges were wrong, and that, after all, is my true opinion, and one I've a right to state. So I'll write no more about it but, like Puddy, I'll say bravely, 'Never mind. She'll try again next year.'

CHAPTER EIGHT

There was a wonderful spell of good weather at the beginning of the holidays. In the mornings all the routine work was carried out as usual, but in the afternoon Margie and Puddy and Fionna went off on expeditions, taking tea and sandwiches with them. Sometimes they went in Florrie, who had not yet been sorted as the garage man in Oban was so busy during the tourist season, and sometimes they went to Iona. But there were occasions when they stayed near

Fionna in the granite quarry. Iona Abbey is in the distance

enough to home for me to slip after them, and although they would have been pleased to see me join them, it amused me to keep out of sight and watch them.

Once they went to a lovely sandy bay not far from the village and they stuffed their frocks inside their panties, and paddled, just like children. There were baby flounders skirmishing in that bay, and you should have heard the yelps when the flicking movements of the tiny fish tickled the legs of one or other of the family. Then when they were tired of paddling, they dammed up one of the streams running into the sea, and you'd be surprised how quickly a big pool formed! Then the dam burst, and the pool vanished, but the sea didn't look any deeper, though it must have been, by an infinitesimal fraction of an inch.

Another time they climbed over to the old granite quarry, and although I had often been there on my own, I did so enjoy going with the family, because I learned things from their conversation that I would never ever have dreamed about.

The red granite of the quarry contrasted beautifully with the purple heather, now in full bloom, and with the gold-tipped leaves of the bracken, which was just beginning to turn bronze. There was a wonderful view at the top of the quarry, across the incredibly blue sea to the green fields and white sands of Iona, with the abbey, which is built of this very same granite, only just discernible against its background of barley and rocks. To the north were the mountains of Mull, across the sea which forms a deep loch almost cutting the island in half, and beyond that, very, very dimly, were the hills of Rum and Skye. South, more sparkling sea, and the twisty rough road climbing over to Erraid, that island made famous in *Kidnapped*. If you haven't read it, read it now. It's by Robert Louis Stevenson, and he was a friend of Kitten's father, so I expect he wrote about David Balfour when he stayed in Mull. Which makes me feel I must read the book again.

Down the steep slope of the quarry, where the truck lines once reached to the now ruined pier, rough steps have been hewn, and on either side were boulders and rejected cuttings of granite, with here and there piles of granite, cut and dressed, ready for shipment overseas. But ships didn't carry them overseas any more. Where once the sound of blasting rent the air, now seagulls wheel and cry, and the cheerful voices of the quarriers no longer echo round the rocks. The closing of the quarries sounded the death knell in the district. The men who once had come here to labour now had to seek elsewhere for work. In time their deserted cottages tumbled down, and, since desolation breeds desolation, even the crofters began to follow suit and sought better amenities and more pay in towns.

So you will understand that even in the bright sunshine there is a sadness lingering in those quarries, and I was glad to hear Margie tell Fionna that it is there, on the summit of the hill, that the bonfire is lighted at times of national rejoicing – Victory Day, a jubilee, a coronation. Then the quarry wakes up again, and people laugh and dance and drink tea and eat dumplings, and it is all the more fun because carrying the stuff up that steep slope has been such a tremendous toil.

If you come to Mull, try to see the quarries. Only twenty minutes' walk across the heather from the village and you're there, and you'll know every second of those twenty minutes has been worth while. And when you're in London, look at Blackfriars Bridge and Holborn Viaduct, for they are built of Mull granite. And don't smile at the Albert Memorial, or call it a hideous Victorian contraption, for it is of Mull granite too.

There is no village hall in Fionnphort, but for many years the village people have been trying to raise money to build one. They have sales of work and concerts and dances, which they hold in the school, but with few people and not very many visitors, raising money is a slow business and gets slower and slower as more people leave the island, either by boat, or in a coffin, if it's not too morbid for me to say so.

I've told you that the Community who are rebuilding around Iona Abbey are also good at helping people. Well, they said they'd help us, and soon there was great activity at the school, where something for the audience to sit on had to be provided and a piano must somehow be found.

The piano was easy, because Kitten and Grandpop said they'd lend the one in the drawing-room. So Archie's lorry came one day, and Archie and lots of other men, including Jimmy-the-Missionary (who belonged to the Community) managed to lift the piano onto the lorry, and off they went while Jimmy-the-Missionary played 'Sing as we go!' with his foot pressed on the hard pedal, so that we could hear him above the sound of the lorry engine all the way to the school.

The seats for the audience were another matter. Planks were placed across empty oil tins, but this was not enough, so benches had to be brought by ferry boat and lorry from Iona. Which will give you an idea of the hardships we face and overcome in a depopulated area like this.

While Jimmy and the men were arranging the big schoolroom for the concert (and Jimmy draped a Union Jack over the piano, which made it look most festive and patriotic) the village women were busy in the small schoolroom preparing tea and sandwiches and cakes for the hundred or so people who would expect supper that night. It's not easy to boil a cauldron of water on a wee primus stove, and it's not easy to produce sandwiches, and to make cakes, when you are not well off and ingredients are scarce. But these women did it, and very well too, as all the people who ate the supper afterwards told one another.

The concert was advertised to begin at eight, because that was the only way to get people to come by half past eight. In fact it was getting on for nine before the audience had collected, arriving by foot from the nearby cottages, and by car from further away. Puddy collected quite a number of people by doing trips back and forth with Florrie, who I am glad to say showed no signs of her petrol trouble. This was luck, and no credit to her since, being inanimate, she doesn't know things like we do.

Some of the audience looked very uncomfortable. These were the ones who arrived too late to sit on one of the benches, so had to be squeezed into the school desks, suitable only for children under eleven, as this was a primary school. I had a good seat myself, on a windowsill, and I didn't attempt to conceal myself, as everyone seemed pleased to have me there and amused that I had decided to come to the concert. Though why it should amuse them I don't know. I've told you before that I'm a musical cat, but of course I hadn't communicated that fact to them.

My word, how I enjoyed that concert! The Community people sang and recited, and even acted little plays which were funny enough to make a human laugh. But it wasn't only the Community people who entertained us, because coming from towns, they couldn't play the bagpipes and they couldn't sing in Gaelic, and our people do like to hear the pipes and the Gaelic songs. So Hughie Lamont came from Bunessan, five miles away, and he brought his pipes, and he wore his kilt, and he played and he sang to us, and as he is very handsome-looking, and has won medals for singing at the Mod, I don't need to tell you how good he was. My word, how the floorboards shook as the people stamped out the rhythm of his tunes, and how the rafters rang as they joined in the chorus of his songs! It was all I could do not to join in myself, singing meow of course, as I haven't got the Gaelic. But I refrained, feeling that I might draw attention to myself, and I never care to be in the public eye.

Towards the end of the concert, dusk was falling, and somebody lighted a paraffin lamp and balanced it on the piano (on which Jimmy-the-Missionary had been playing accompaniments all evening) in what I considered was a very precarious way. But don't be alarmed. There wasn't a terrible fire disaster or anything like that. The people here know how to manage lamps all right, though they seem so vague about them.

The grand finale (from the *Petit Dictionnaire*) was when all the entertainers stood on the platform together and sang 'The Old Folks at Home' in beautiful harmony. Somehow I couldn't turn my thoughts to Ealing, where I suppose they should have been, but I felt very sentimental all the same, and looking around the room, I knew that the people were thinking of their old folks, some of whom I expect had been dead for years.

It took only a few minutes to pack away the benches, which had taken hours to arrange, and very soon Hughie was tuning his pipes and Johnnie-the-Master-of-Ceremonies was shouting out, 'Take your partners for the eightsome reel!' I had stayed quietly on my windowsill, and someone had now put a lamp up beside me, so that I felt rather illuminated, but it didn't stop my enjoyment of the dancing, and now and again I ventured a wee 'hooch', which nobody would hear, as they were all hooching their throats hoarse. The floorboards shook and the paraffin lamps quivered on their hooks, but they didn't fall down.

By midnight everyone was tired and thirsty after their exertions, for even the ones who were too old and stiff to dance had been tapping out the rhythm with their feet. The tea emerged from the side room, with a tray of cups and a huge teapot, and milk and sugar. And others followed, carrying trays piled high with sandwiches and cakes. What a feast! Soon everyone had eaten all they wanted, and even I had not been neglected, as Fionna, who was helping to hand things round, had given me a delicious helping of salmon out of a sandwich.

When all the dishes had been cleared away, the family said 'Good night' and slipped off home, as was the custom. But I stayed on, right up to the end, and I stood up like everyone else, when Jimmy played 'God Save the Queen'.

It's surprising how quickly everyone disappeared for home. Archie and his lorry provided transport for all the Community from Iona, and cars gave people lifts to their various homes. So soon I was alone on the road, feeling a very small cat, and I had to walk carefully, as it must have rained heavily at some time during the evening. The moonlight shimmered on the loch, and now the moon was here, now gone, and black clouds were scudding across its face. A rat ran across my path, but I ignored it. I was glad to see the huge white gate of home gleaming, and I slipped under it, up the drive, to my bed in the electric-lighting plant house.

The house was warm, and the engine creaked from time to time, as it always did when it was cooling down after being used. The family only switched it on now for special occasions, as it burnt petrol, which is so much more expensive than the paraffin needed by lamps.

I curled up on the old red hospital blanket, specially there for me, and soon I was fast asleep and I didn't know anything more until Carla bounced in on me to call me in the morning.

CHAPTER NINE

It isn't often that Margie's summer holiday coincides with Fionna's birthday, but it did this time, which was a lucky thing, as Fionna loves to have all the family together when one of them is having a birthday so that none of them misses the fun. So as she watched Kitten making the birthday cake, which was a layer cake in

Grandpop with Arnish and Flora outside the engine house

three different colours, since that is her favourite kind, she chatted about John, and how especially much she would miss him at her birthday tea, and how she would like to send him some of the cake when it was iced. But Kitten explained that this sort of cake became stale very quickly.

So they decided that next year, if John was still away, they'd make a rich fruit cake instead, which would travel better. So that was settled.

Fionna's birthday presents were always placed in the very same Moses basket that had been her first cradle when she was born. And when she woke up, she would carry the basket to Kitten and Grandpop's room, where the family would sing 'Happy Birthday' before watching her open her presents. And I must tell you that Fionna was just as excited over other people's birthdays as she was over her own, and when it was she singing 'Happy Birthday' instead of being sung to, she put so much spirit in it that would ensure the lucky person being happy for days and days.

The birthday cake looked just lovely, with its candles lighted (Puddy had drawn the curtain to make the dining-room dark), and there were meringues and all Fionna's other favourite things for tea. And the family sang 'Happy Birthday' all over again, although her birthday only had a few hours left by now. And soon, almost too soon after tea, there was the birthday dinner, with one of the brown Rhode Island hens that hadn't laid for ages made into a casserole, as she was too tough to roast.

And that night John telephoned from Stirling Castle and sang 'Happy Birthday' twice through in spite of the pips. So Fionna felt almost as if he had been with her after all. And she thought it the nicest birthday she had ever had. A thought, I may say, she somehow seems to have every year.

Before Margie returned to London, she helped to bring in the hay, raking it up after Puddy had cut it down with the cutter attachment on Puffing Billy and forming it first into little stooks, and then, helped by Puddy and Fionna and Grandpop, into big ricks. Fionna's job was to stand on top of the rick, receiving the hay the others tossed up to her, and bouncing on it, to compress it and make room for more. It was a wonderful job, and she made the most of it. Sitting quietly nearby, I was sometimes afraid she would bounce right off and land on the ground. But she didn't.

There were also the peats, which had been cut earlier in the year, to be brought in from the peat moss behind the house. These were stacked near the back door, and the family had to carry them in sacks on their backs as Corrie wasn't here, with her panniers, to do the job for them.

One of the ducks and one of the drakes helped to make Margie's last supper at home a gala occasion. I don't know if 'helped' is the right word, because it implies free will and desire on the part of the helper, and I'm afraid there was no free will about the ducks' presence that night. Indeed, they protested loudly when Grandpop caught them and tied up their legs, and handed them over to Johnnie-the-Postman who obligingly acted as poultry executioner in the district. It was a convenient arrangement, as he delivered the letters, then wrung the bird's neck, so he didn't have to make a special visit. Doing it in the course of his work made the whole thing less morbid, except, perhaps, for the victim. However, he was skilled at the job, so I don't suppose it hurt, though I'm glad it won't ever happen to me. It's a mercy people don't eat cats.

Green peas and apple sauce traditionally go with duck, and so they did that night. And Puddy made excellent meringues, which Kitten filled with goat's cream. And Carla and I were not forgotten. So the whole evening went well and was a memorable occasion.

I'm afraid I overslept the next morning, so I did not see Margie leave by the mail bus, which passes our gate at 7.15 a.m. That is a very early hour at which to start a journey, and the bus would bump over the rough roads for nearly two hours before arriving at Craignure, from which the brave little *Lochinvar* would take the travellers to Oban, and thence to the four corners of the world – that is if they wanted to, and could find corners in a world the books in the cottage assure me is round.

That is a very long sentence, and because the *Lochinvar* is of supreme importance to the people in Mull, I feel that I must pause to tell you a little about her.

I've never seen the *Queen Elizabeth* or the *Queen*

Mary, or any of the huge ocean-going ships, though the *Caronia* sometimes comes to Oban, with very rich tourists from America, who buy all the tweed and woollens from the Oban shops and leave lots of dollars behind. But that is to diverge. What I'm trying to say is that compared with big ships, the *Lochinvar* is very small indeed. It carries mail and passengers and animals and cars between Oban and Tobermory daily, and although it is a little ship, the sea is often just as rough as it is for the big ships, so to my mind the *Lochinvar* and all her crew deserve a big George Cross to hang on her little artificial funnel.

The passengers from Craignure could do with a little official recognition, too, because since there is no pier at Craignure they have to scramble into a motor boat, which transports them to the *Lochinvar*, then they have to scramble out of the motor boat and on to the *Lochinvar*, often in very heavy seas, so that this is no mean feat, especially for old or corpulent people. (According to the grammar books in the cottage, the word 'fat' would be better English, but I think corpulent sounds more grand.)

The building of a pier at Craignure is one of the chief topics of discussion, and grumbles, on the island, and I understand has been so for years. I wouldn't like to be a county councillor. It must be so hopeless to convince people that what is desirable may not be financially possible. All the same, I hope that if the ferry boat one day sinks, none of my family will be on it.

I pictured Margie bobbing across the water with

the luggage and the mail bags, and maybe a live calf or two, neatly parcelled up in sacks, and I hoped her wound wouldn't split open when she jumped onto the *Lochinvar*. It couldn't have done, or I'd have heard.

Soon after Margie left, a very sad thing happened indeed. I have told you about the succulent grass that grows at the edge of the bog, and how afraid I was that Corrieshellach might one day eat too eagerly of it and sink into the bog too deeply to be able to struggle out. Well, just that very same thing happened to poor Iain, who, with Peter, had been grazing out on the common with a herd of cattle he had made friends with. Nobody knows how it happened for, like Corrie, he had inherited an awareness of danger about bogs, but one morning his poor swollen body was found, deeply imbedded, and it was clear that the more he had struggled to free himself, the deeper he had sunk in. It took seven men to pull him out and bury him, for his carcass was no use as meat, since he had been drowned.

Perhaps you wonder how, with so few people about, it was possible to find some able-bodied men to carry out this job, so I'll remind you that this is the Highlands, and although nobody lights beacons or anything like that to summon help, somehow word gets around, and in next to no time willing helpers gather together, ready to toil till they drop in order to give a hand to anyone in trouble.

So it was only Peter who went to the Bunessan cattle sale that autumn, and although he fetched a good price, the death of Iain had been a bad financial loss to

Puddy, whose finances were never up to much at the best of times. All the same, it was not the Savings Certificates she couldn't buy that bothered Puddy; it was the thought that poor Iain had come to such a horrible end. Puddy is too sentimental to be a successful farmer, so if ever she makes any money, it will need to be with the pools.

Soon after Fionna returned to school, Puddy went away for her annual holiday. This chapter is full of people going away, but it can't be helped, since I am writing a true account of the family, and not a fiction. Puddy's annual holiday took place in October, and she chose it then so that she could go to the Horse of the Year Show in London. I have spoken of it before, because of Corrieshellach's ambitions to go there, but I'll write of it again, even though you may accuse me of advertising it. That show gives Puddy so much pleasure that I'm sure it deserves all the good things I can say about it. Anyhow, go to it yourself and see for yourself.

Writing about Puddy's annual holiday makes it sound as if she only went away once a year. Of course she doesn't. She has a week away here and there, sometimes taking Fionna back to school, or going to some special parties, or to an extra horse show. She says it's good to get the ashes out of her hair and wear party frocks again, and I must say she must collect up a good deal of ash, because with all the fires we have, a whole tin tub-load goes out every day, and no matter which way the wind is blowing, or how careful Puddy is, when she tips them away they all seem to blow back on her.

Carla is very sad when Puddy goes. She sits on the oak chest by the dining-room window all day long, watching for her to come back. But by the next day she decides waiting is no use, so she follows round after Grandpop, and soon is quite happy again.

With Puddy away, Grandpop takes care of the goats and does the milking – not very easy since the milking stool is very low and stooping is sore on his back. But the goats do well under his care, for he is never done feeding them. I must admit that he is also never done feeding me. I have only to look up at him wistfully, and he says, 'Nicholas, the poor cat!' and puts some food in my dish. He also feeds Carla on tit-bits at every meal, and since she has no pride in her appearance she will soon not be a bitch but a bolster.

Kitten was in charge of the hens, and these fully justified all the care they had had as chickens. But I can't say I care for hens. All day long they quarrel and sometimes even fight, and although they lay good, big eggs, they have neither charm nor intelligence. The ducks, on the other hand, are most amiable creatures, obviously enjoying life to its full, which is as well, since all are destined so soon to go to the pot.

Puddy returned, talking happily of Foxhunter and Tosca and all the other lovely horses she had seen, and Carla at once forsook Grandpop, which I thought was tactless and unfeeling of her, and I consider he took it in very good part, for he still stuffed her with snacks. It was frosty now, and the crofters were shaking their heads because they hadn't lifted their potatoes, and the frost would ruin any that were not well buried in the ground.

In this frosty weather the loch looked like a mirror, and every day a flock of geese would fly over us from somewhere to somewhere. I have seen Puddy outside, gazing up entranced at the sight of the wonderful formation flying. And, indeed, I feel a thrill myself at times when on a crisp sunny morning the beat of their wings and their strange cry echoes across the water. The swans, too, were back, sometimes for a day or so, sometimes for a week. I must find a book about geese and swans, then I'll know just what they do when they are not with us.

Puddy was kept busy with her veterinary medicines, which she kept in a cupboard in the scullery. Arnish had punctured an udder one day, when she climbed over some barbed wire over which she had no right to climb. Her milk was trickling out of the hole, and I am sure she must have been in pain. But soon Puddy noticed what had happened, and after bathing the sore place with disinfectant, she covered it with sticking plaster. And she milked Arnish oh, so gently, that Arnish felt no pain at all, and very soon she was well again and Puddy pulled off the plaster so skilfully that even that didn't hurt.

Seeing how careful Puddy was with Arnish gave me great confidence when, a while later, I suffered some mishap myself. A deep wound in my chest, brought about in an unfortunate encounter with another cat, became septic, and a nasty abscess formed. At the same time I contracted a horrid itch on one leg, which, since I licked it, soon caused my skin to become raw and oozing. Puddy cut a wide collar of cardboard, which she tied round my neck so that I could not lick, however hard I tried, and she bathed my sore leg with stuff out of one bottle, and she bathed the sore chest with stuff out of another bottle; and very soon both my leg and chest were completely cured and have not troubled me since. And the cardboard collar, which might have caused me great fear, had I not known and trusted Puddy, is neatly put in the veterinary cupboard, in case it should be needed again. But I'm resolved to be more careful next time.

If I used chapter headings, I would call this one 'Farewells and Accidents' and perhaps have a little quotation underneath, which I think very grand, and which I intend to use in my next book. So I'll end this with the biggest farewell of all, which came to us one night by telephone. It was from John. His regiment was suddenly ordered to an outpost of the Empire (yes, I mean Empire; I'm a conservative cat) and he was to leave Britain at once, to put a stop to any trouble that might have started, or to scare the troublemakers into not starting at all. There was no time for embarkation leave, no time for anything but this hurried goodbye.

And how long would he be away? Kitten yelled down the phone, for the line was very bad, as it often is here. There was no telling. Perhaps three years. It all depended on what the regiment had to do when they got there.

And that, on a muffled and fading telephone call, was to be the last we would hear of John's cheerful voice. For how long? Perhaps forever. I've been in a few scraps myself, and I know.

Chapter Ten

One good thing came out of John's posting to Overseas Services. As soon as it was known that the Communists were responsible for the trouble he was going to quell, Arnish stopped all her Communist talk, and soon you'd think she'd been true-blue Conservative all her days. Arnish loved John dearly, and the thought that he might be in danger from the very people she had so often praised, caused her both shame and anxiety. I could hear her telling Flora how easily one could be misled in political affairs, and how careful Flora must be in future before she reached an opinion and lauded any political party of any kind.

Achaban House

You'd think that it was Flora who had been the Fellow Traveller, the way Arnish talked! And I think poor Flora was quite ready to believe so herself, by the time Arnish had finished. Anyhow, she became very quiet and subdued, and would give way to Arnish over any fancied tit-bit without so much as an attempt at a butting-match. And so Arnish not only cleared her own conscience but established her position as Flora's superior.

But Arnish could not go for long without laying down the law on something, and one day when Grandpop was having a bonfire just outside the back gate, she grabbed from the flames a book about Madeira, which someone had received from a travel agency. Of course she ate it, but before she ate it she read a whole lot of information about the glorious sunshine, and the flowers, visitors to the island would enjoy. Soon she was endlessly extolling the virtues of a sunny climate, and of Madeira in particular, to Flora, and I would hear the pair of them, at night, after they had been fed and milked, chewing the cud and discussing the desirability of emigration to such a clime.

Of course it was all talk and no do, as it always was with the goats. And as I sat outside their house and overheard what they were saying – for of course I was not listening, but only happening to hear – I thought how easy it would be for a cat to emigrate, but how difficult for a goat! Nobody would think it remarkable if a cat stalked up the gangway of a ship, and settled himself as a member of the crew. But a goat, never!

And I was greatly comforted by the thought, for though I knew this was only silly talk, it did occur to me how very sad it would be for Puddy to come one day and find that the goats had left her. And I don't know how Kitten would manage without their milk.

However, it was not long before both of the goats had more important things to talk about. It was the mating season now, for goats mate during the winter, and Puddy knew by the plaintive sound of their 'baas', and by the wagging of their tails, when Arnish and Flora were calling for 'Billy'. There was no billy near, but there was one five miles away, along a very bumpy and out-of-the-way road. Florrie doesn't mind bumpy roads, because cars aren't made so they mind things at all, so one day Puddy took the back seat out of Florrie, and she put some sacks down where the seat had been, and then she put down a bundle of hay, and soon she had coaxed Arnish to climb into Florrie to nibble the hay. And off they went to the outlandish place, with the blue smoke pouring out of Florrie's exhaust, and a few hours later back they came, with Arnish looking very smug and with Puddy full of praise for the way everything had gone, including Florrie, who, in spite of the ominous blue smoke and the rattle of the engine, had not once stopped, except when Puddy made her.

I don't know what Arnish told Flora about her adventure, but a few weeks later Flora made such a to-do about looking for Billy that Puddy brought out the back seat of Florrie all over again, and put down the sacks, and finally drove off with Flora. But this time

Florrie didn't behave well and stopped several times, and when Puddy arrived home she was so annoyed with Florrie that she didn't say what had gone on with Flora. So I don't know whether she had behaved herself or not.

Now all the talk in the goat-house was of kids. Arnish wanted a billy, and Flora wanted a nanny, and they were never done telling each other so. But I knew Puddy didn't want any billies about because he would not be pure bred (since the father was a Brown Toggenburg, not a British Sanaan), so she could not keep him for breeding purposes, and a billy is no use for anything else. This would mean that Willie Campbell, who is a butcher as well as a farmer, would have to come along with his humane killer, and that would be the end of the baby billy.

I said nothing of this to Arnish of course. And for her sake, as well as for Puddy's, I hoped she would not get what she desired.

The darkness fell earlier and earlier, and there was less to do outside. The bracken was bronze-coloured now, and the fields were a misty shade of gold. The harvest was in, and the garden needed nothing now but rest. Puddy would go out every day with her little gun, and in next to no time she'd be back with a rabbit, for she is a very good shot, and rabbits were very plentiful indeed. But suddenly the rabbits seemed to vanish, though Puddy could not possibly have killed them all.

Soon somebody was able to give the reason for this. A polecat had come to live near us! Now rabbits are terrified of polecats, and so, I confess, am I. The hens would be terrified too, had they the wit to know of their new neighbour, for polecats are very partial to hens, but somehow the word never got round to them, and Puddy shut them up so securely at night that no marauder could get at them. So although the tufts of fur lying about the place indicated the number of rabbits that had fallen victim, the hens remained immune and unaware of these attacks.

Inside the house, Kitten was busy making Christmas cakes and Christmas puddings. She had bought the ingredients for these in the village post-office-cum-stores, and I assure you that the very grandest grocers in London don't have better groceries than does our village shop. Of course, you can't buy things like chicken-in-aspic there, for who would want chicken-in-aspic when they can have a nice fresh hen from their own back yard? But as well as currants and raisins and flour and other edible things, you can buy shampoo and writing paper and lamps and string and all manner of things besides. Everything in the shop is fresh and polished, and Betty-and-her-Mother, who own the shop, will do things for you that you'll never get done in the grand towny shops. They'll ring you up and tell you if something specially nice is in. They'll tell you when you must send in your National Health card, and how many stamps you'll need for it, and that you'll be in trouble if you don't renew Carla's licence (just imagine her having to have a licence, like a radio or a gun! I consider it most demeaning).

Indeed, but for Betty-and-her-Mother, I don't know where the family would be, and I'm sure they don't know either. And I'd like to say here that until not very long ago it used to be Betty-and-her-Mother-and-her-Father who did all these things. The father was called Johnnie, and there was not a family joy, or a family sorrow, or a family trouble, that he was not told about at once. And because he was such a friend and adviser of the people I love, I feel he must be included in my book, and that I must state how sad they all were that he is not smiling behind the counter any more.

The early Christmas preparations didn't interest me much. Carla would temporarily forsake Puddy to sit pop-eyed and whimpering on the floor, willing Kitten to toss her the odd raisin or stray bit of dough. But I remained happily curled up by the fire in the wee sitting room, watching Grandpop filling in his pools coupons or nodding gently over his book. Indeed, it would be Christmas Day itself before my interest was really roused, for though I find a bit of raw chicken very tasty, I knew my family would not give me any until it was cooked. So I waited in patience and did not even evince interest in the discussion about which two hens were to furnish the main course of the Christmas dinner. I've said before, as personalities I find the hens a bore, and which one gets its neck wrung, and when, is a matter of indifference to me.

As a matter of fact it turned out that instead of two hens it was a turkey that graced the table that Christmas Day. Kitten went to the mainland to fetch

Fionna from school, and when she returned she had a huge turkey with her as well as Fionna. So the hens had a reprieve, but as they didn't know they had been sentenced to death, they experienced no sense of relief at all.

With the arrival of Fionna, things really did get busy. Puddy and Fionna set off in Florrie to the little plantation two miles up the road, and when they returned, Florrie looked more like a mechanical forest than a car, for branches of trees were tied all over her. Soon these trees were placed in tubs, one in our drawing-room and one in the church, and Fionna and Puddy decorated them most beautifully so that they sparkled and shone and gave a real air of gladness, which of course is just how it should be at Christmas, one of the happiest seasons of the year.

Margie was arriving on Christmas Eve, so of course her bedroom had been getting prepared ever since the first pudding went into the pot, and long before the Christmas cake, with its white icing and gay decorations, was placed on the sideboard in the dining-room.

Johnnie-the-Postman was laden every evening, delivering stacks of cards and heaps of parcels. The cards were opened and hung on string across the dining-room and drawing-room (this is a very gay effect, and better than arranging them on tables, where they have to be removed for dusting). The parcels, however, were hidden away by anyone to whom they were not addressed, for no presents are opened until Christmas Day by our family.

I noticed with some pleasure that there was a parcel on the Christmas tree for me. I guessed by its shape that it was probably 'Katteo', but I've always been brought up to appreciate the thought rather than the gift. There was a parcel, too, for Carla, and I guessed it was a rubber ball. There was also a parcel which puzzled me very much. It was very small and bore a huge label on which was written the one word, 'Lottie'.

Who on earth was Lottie?

I cleaned my paws, and racked my brains, but could not place that name at all.

But when Christmas Eve came, I knew.

CHAPTER ELEVEN

By half past four the electric-light plant was humming, and Fionna had switched on every light in the house, because that is the sign of a Highland welcome.

As I walked up the drive the frosty earth was cold under my paws and my legs were feeling rather stiff because, being Christmas Eve, I had felt it my duty to

Lottie and Nicky

visit my various families to wish them the compliments of the season.

The Christmas tree in the bay window of the drawing-room looked wonderfully festive, its branches laden with sparkling balls and gaily wrapped parcels. Because of the illuminations, I could see Puddy and Fionna standing by the window above, which was Kitten's bedroom, and I knew they were watching for the glimmering light, away in the darkness, that would indicate the approach of the mail bus. And in the bus would be Margie.

I sat for a while outside the drawing-room window, but although the fire burnt cheerfully within, no one was there. Kitten would be busy in the kitchen, for she knew that after that long, cold, drive there was nothing more welcoming than a good hot meal, and Grandpop would be watching for the bus from his office window, thinking, perhaps, that Puddy and Fionna would be chattering so much together they'd not notice it until too late.

So, since nobody would notice me and let me in, I settled down for a chilly nap. It was the sound of Puddy and Fionna's voices that awakened me. They were running down the drive, flashing a torch, and just in time to see the mail bus draw up at the gate.

I slipped into the house, for Grandpop had left the door open when he followed the others down the drive, and I awaited the arrival of Margie with dignity, sitting on the sofa.

But when the drawing-room door, which was ajar,

was pushed open, it was not any of the family that entered the room. It was – what? A queer little black animal, about the same size as me, with funny bushy whiskers, a stiff black tail, just like a wee black mop, and the queerest animal legs I have ever seen – I thought at first it must be wearing high heels.

I am afraid I gave the newcomer a very unfriendly reception. I arched my back and spat, then, remembering my manners, and realising that these tactics had made the queer thing withdraw a couple of paces, I asked, 'Who are you?' And even as I spoke, I realised what the creature was, for I had seen pictures like it in Puddy's animal books. It was a French poodle! In some alarm, my thoughts flew to the *Petit Dictionnaire* in the cottage, and I wondered if I would have to address this creature in French, and if I had learnt enough French phrases to be able to hold my own in such an event. But as these thoughts flashed through my head, the strange visitor put me at ease.

'I'm Lottie,' she said. 'I'm Margie's poodle. And I've come for Christmas.' And later I was to learn that her soft sing-song accent had nothing French about it, for Lottie had been born in Shropshire, right on the border with Wales, and the time she had spent in London had not eradicated her soft, lilting tongue.

It was soon obvious that Lottie was going to be the centre of attention for as long as she stayed, and in fairness to her I must say at once that this did not go to her head. She was a most amiable creature, who had nothing but good to say to everyone and everything, and I'm sure you'll agree that that in itself is a most refreshing characteristic.

Carla, I am afraid, showed up very badly at first against Lottie. I don't know what came over her, for though Lottie's appearance was certainly odd, nobody could say she looked vicious. Yet Carla was clearly afraid of her and would make a wide circle round her, if ever she had to pass her. Lottie, who was all for being friendly, must have found this most bewildering.

I tried to make peace between the two by explaining to Carla that, though they differed in appearance, she and Lottie were, after all, the same type of animal. To my surprise Lottie interrupted this wise statement by saying, with some asperity, 'Look you, there is clearly some misunderstanding in your mind! Poodles are not dogs. They are quite different. There are many kinds of animals, and I do not need to list them all. But to explain what I mean, I'll tell you there are lions and tigers and elephants and camels and cats and dogs and poodles and mice!' And with that she realised that her beloved Margie had left the room, so with a leap into the air, she bounded off after her.

Carla, I could see, was perplexed, and I realised that she had never even heard of lions and tigers and all the strange names that Lottie had reeled off so glibly.

'Don't worry, Carla,' I said, 'Lottie lives in London, so I've no doubt she has stored a great deal of knowledge in her head. But I'm quite sure she's wrong about poodles, only don't hurt her feelings by telling her so.'

Carla, I am glad to say, took heed of my suggestion, for during the stay I often heard Lottie repeating her rigmarole about lions and tigers and elephants and camels and dogs and cats and poodles and mice, and never once did Carla suggest that she was wrong, though she must have wanted to many a time. After that, Carla went up in my estimation. I never would have credited her with so much self-control. Which shows how wrong one can be about our judgement of others, even of those we live with.

Lottie has caused a diversion in my chronicle, just as she did in our daily life. That first evening, while Carla and Lottie and I were getting to know one another, the family were busily engaged in doing mysterious things with coloured paper and string behind closed doors, in their various bedrooms. Calls of 'Don't come in!' and 'Don't look at present!' echoed round the house, and although Lottie was puzzled, for this was her first Christmas, I knew that all this meant that everyone was doing up the presents they had bought for each other, a task which they somehow always left until the eleventh hour.

Kitten had put out five pillow-cases, one for each member of the family, and when bedtime came, there would be a pillow-case at the end of every bed. They wouldn't stay empty for long, because it didn't need Midnight and Father Christmas to cause these pillow-cases to bulge. I'm not going to write a treatise on the Father Christmas legend, for maybe you are either a bitter cynic or a firm believer in that benevolent bewhiskered gentleman. And far be it from me to disillusion you. But I'll say this. It is a historical fact that just such a gentleman did provide gifts to his fellow men, and perhaps to children in particular, and while he may not now run a kind of celestial factory, I'm sure he must smile to see how his beneficence still infects the actions of millions of people.

Lottie was taking a great interest in Kitten's activities in the kitchen, and I soon found that this was because the turkey was being stuffed. Now, the stuffing Kitten puts into a fowl is the most delicious I have ever tasted. It is made of oatmeal and chopped onions, mixed up with fat, and of course seasoned with salt and pepper. Do try it, and you'll never revert to sage and onion again. I think Lottie was very disappointed when the plump, and now stuffed, bird was returned to the larder, but I explained to her that tomorrow evening it would be the oven, and not the larder, for that turkey. And when it came out, all brown and sizzling, we'd get our share, never fear. Lottie was of a trusting nature, and I knew she believed me and wouldn't worry. Indeed, already I felt a certain affinity with this odd black poodle. And only a couple of hours ago, I had spat at her! Even as I write, I blush!

You must be wondering why it is I haven't written of Corrieshellach for so long. The truth is that writing about her depresses me. No, there is nothing wrong with her, so don't worry, but I had thought that when she returned from the Royal Highland Show we would have a great welcome ready for her, with the flag up and banners, and an extra feed of oats. For as I've said before, third prize at a big show like that is very good indeed, and, anyway, all of us who know her know that it should have been a first.

However, my daydreams about her return were soon confounded, for I heard Puddy say one day that she had decided that it was wiser to leave Corrie on the mainland until after the foal had arrived. And Puddy put it in such a firm way, that I know she would not change her mind.

Disappointed though I was, and lonely too, I was glad that Corrie really was having a foal, for a beautiful and noble pony like that certainly needs to be perpetuated. And one day a collie dog belonging to one of our local farmers came to me and told me that he'd been over with his master to a cattle sale at Perth, and there he had met a collie who belonged to the very farm where Corrie was now living. And thinking he might meet a dog that would know me, Corrie had had the good sense to give him a message for me. She said she missed me and all our family very much, but was very well cared for where she was living, and when she came home she'd have her foal with her, which would be a happier return even than winning the Supreme Championship. So now you know as much about Corrie as I do, and you'll know, too, how we animals manage to get word one to another. And it doesn't even cost us a postage stamp!

I was a bit sorry that there was no snow that night, as Lottie had an idea that Christmas Day and snow went together, like thunder and lightning or strawberries and cream. But I suppose she'll need to learn one day, and the sooner the better. Anyhow, it was a crisp night with a very starry sky, and as far as I know, that first Christmas might have been just the very same, in spite of the pictures on the Christmas cards.

I paid a midnight visit to Arnish and Flora. They were very subdued that night because all farm animals are mindful of the important part their ancestors played around that manger in Bethlehem. I didn't stay long. When hearts are full, there is no need for words.

Grandpop had rearranged my blanket in the engine house. It was all fluffed up and very soft. I think that thoughtfulness was one of my nicest Christmas presents.

The house was silent now; the family asleep. And very soon, so was I.

Chapter Twelve

Anyone switching on a light automatically starts up the electric engine, which is a very clever idea, but a very alarming one if one is a cat and happens to sleep in the engine house. So the unexpected throbbing woke me up with a start, and it was a minute before I realised that this was Christmas Day, and Puddy was making the early morning tea in electric light instead of lamp light. I've told you before that petrol being the price it is, the electric plant is only used on special occasions.

Carla

I heard the back door open, so I quickly jumped out of bed, and shot to the house, just as Lottie and Carla bounded out to attend to their first duty of the day. They accorded me a warm, somewhat rough, greeting, and Puddy received me in the kitchen with a nice Christmas cuddle and, better still, a dish of warm milk.

When she had made the tea, Puddy and Carla and Lottie disappeared upstairs, and I knew that all the family would gather in Grandpop and Kitten's room and drink their morning tea and open the presents from their pillowcases. I could hear the chink of cups and saucers and a lot of laughter, and now and again I caught the word 'John', and this made me feel rather sad. I realised that all over the world people would be laughing and opening presents today, and in many, many homes behind the laughter would be a sorrow that someone they loved was far away.

I expect John was opening parcels too in his remote corner of the Empire, for I know that a lot of parcels had been sent to him, neatly stitched up in cotton, bearing a label on which was a list of the contents of the parcels, and their value. I know the Authorities demand this, but I think it's a pity to spoil the excitement of opening a parcel by having what's inside written on the label. Don't you? So I hoped John hadn't read those labels, which bore socks (11/- a pair) shirts (£2 10/- each. Incidentally, what an iniquitous price for plain, white cotton!) Books (various prices) and fudge (2 lbs, home made). This latter, I need hardly tell you, was from Kitten.

Anyhow, whether he read them or not, John would laugh a lot, for he is always laughing. I wish I knew what time his clocks would say it was while ours said what they did. This clock business is a puzzle and an inconvenience when one tries to think of absent friends doing things at the time we are doing them ourselves. Such as eating.

I was sitting by my empty dish, brooding about John, when Puddy came back to the kitchen to fill the teapot with more water. When she had done this, she tucked me under her arm and took me upstairs, and what a sight met my eyes in Kitten and Grandpop's room! There was paper everywhere. Brown paper, white paper, multi-coloured paper, tissue paper, and paper which I thought much too pretty to wrap things up in at all. And it didn't help that Lottie and Carla, who had apparently developed a benevolent Christmas Spirit, were romping around together, pulling at paper here, and chewing at string there. I picked my way carefully to a spot near dear Grandpop, and although I pretended to go to sleep, I was all ears for the happy voices of the family.

And what do you think John had sent Fionna? A pair of silver filigree earrings, the very first earrings she had ever had and, because it was Christmas, she was allowed to wear them that day, though really she wouldn't be old enough to wear them for years.

It was a lovely start to a lovely day. When the room was cleared up, as it was almost miraculously by Margie, and the usual morning chores finished, I followed the family to church and I was able to peep inside and see the Christmas tree, also the golden blossomed whin and the brightly berried holly with which Puddy had decorated the Communion table and window sills.

The family would be quite happy to have me with them in their pew, but in case other families had less enlightened ideas, I thought it best to remain outside during the service. Huddled where I was in a corner of the porch, I felt chilly, for the wind was bitingly cold, but my heart was warmed by the singing of those lovely Christmas hymns – and by the cosy voice of the minister, who was telling the people the Christmas story. I have often listened outside that church, but most of all I like listening at Christmas, and when I returned home later, I still had the strains of 'Come all ye Faithful' ringing in my ears. But I'm afraid not nearly all the Faithful had come, for there were not many people at church. I would feel very privileged to be allowed to attend a service. I wish people could feel that as well.

Lunch consisted of coffee and sandwiches, as usual, but for tea there was a great array of scones and pancakes, with of course the big Christmas cake, but although she had prepared such delicious fare, Kitten warned the family that, with dinner only a few hours off – and what a dinner! – they must not eat too much.

It was after tea that Fionna distributed the presents from the Christmas tree. As I had suspected, my present proved to be 'Katteo', prettily wrapped up in holly-patterned paper. I resolved that when the time came I would eat up that Katteo with every show of pleasure. I wouldn't like the family to feel their gift to me was not appreciated. I am an affectionate cat and I like to please.

Lottie and Carla had a grand time, chasing round the house after their new balls. I think that given the chance Lottie would be excellent at the game of billiards. She has a most remarkable aim when she pushes her ball with her nose. Poor Lottie! She had been in trouble during the afternoon, for she unfortu-nately felt playful during the Queen's speech, and when Lottie feels playful, she nips at people's ankles to indicate to them that they should feel playful too. So Lottie was eventually banished to the kitchen, from whence her protesting yelps punctuated the beautiful and gracious words of Her Majesty. I am a loyal and patriotic cat, and I deplored Lottie's lack of respect. But of course she is only a puppy, and she'll learn.

Dinner came at last. Scotch broth, followed by the turkey, perfectly cooked and nicely browned, and dished up with all manner of trimmings. But since these are not of prime importance to me, I did not particularly observe what they were. Finally there was the plum-pudding, with a gay piece of holly sticking out of it, and flames all around it. This caused me momentary alarm, but I soon realised that the flames were intentional, as Puddy said she thought it a waste to set fire to brandy.

There were buttons and three-penny bits, and all

sorts of things in the pudding, besides fruits, but these were for keeping and not for eating, and the finding of them was evidently of some significance. Anyway, it caused much amusement, especially when Margie accidentally swallowed a button.

I said the pudding was final, but of course it wasn't, because there were sweets, and nuts and fruit yet to be eaten, and crackers to be pulled (to poor Lottie's distress), and so the table that had looked so gay looked very messy, with torn pieces of paper and tangerine peel and broken nutshells.

While Puddy and Margie did the washing up, Kitten gave Lottie and Carla and me our share of the dinner. How very tasty is turkey! I savoured every morsel before I ate it, and so I was eating long after the others had finished their share. I wonder why dogs (and poodles) eat so fast? Will they never realise that anticipation is better than realisation? However, although two pairs of eyes were fixed on me, and, I'm afraid, grudging me every mouthful, I ate my dinner with quiet dignity, cleaned myself nicely when I had done, and then I joined the family in the drawing-room, and I settled down on Grandpop's knee for a nice after-dinner nap.

Fortunately, as soon as Christmas is over, people here have the New Year to look forward to. And particularly is this true of our family, for to Highland Kitten, Hogmanay (as New Year's Eve is called) is the most important night of the year. Indeed, Boxing Day had seen the last of the ducks, for Johnnie-the-Postman had acted executioner for the last time that year, and the victims had now been dispatched in parcels to those of Kitten's relations who lived in cities, so couldn't keep Hogmanay ducks for themselves.

On New Year's Day we, too, would eat duck, and somehow the idea didn't much appeal to me. Not that I had managed to become friendly with the ducks, who, to their bitter end, had always been afraid of everyone. All the same, I'd felt a certain affection for them, unlike my attitude to hens, and I didn't feel that I'd enjoy eating them any more than I enjoyed Katteo. As a matter of fact, time proved me wrong in this, for as soon as I got my teeth into that tasty bit of wing I forgot all about it being duck.

Humans 'bring in' the New Year. That is, they sit up, no matter how sleepy they are, and at twelve o'clock sharp they wish one another a Happy New Year, and they drink a toast to absent friends and to the future. My family do, anyhow.

So on New Year's Eve we all sat in the drawing-room and listened to the radio, and on a table was a decanter and glasses and shortbread, because the family eat the New Year in as well. And there wasn't a lot of conversation, because Lottie and Carla were asleep, and I knew that all the others were thinking about the year that was past, which had sometimes been happy and sometimes sad, like most years are for most people, and I knew, too, that Puddy in particular would think back to other years and wish that she could forget about Fionna's father, instead of thinking about him every day of every year, and especially now. And of course they were all also thinking of John, who had sent them the Happy New Year telegram which was now propped up on the mantelpiece.

I am glad to say that the trouble in that outpost of the Empire hadn't turned into anything serious after all, and I'm quite sure that it was the arrival of that splendid Highland regiment, with its tough-looking men wearing kilts and dirks, and a determined expression, which had made the troublemakers change their minds. There aren't many folks would care to take on the Highlanders in a fight, and unless I am much mistaken, the Communists are better at stirring up trouble than they are at fighting a battle. So John was safe, and enjoying life abroad, just as he always enjoyed life at home. Inside myself I wished him a happy New Year, and a speedy return, and if I had the gift of tears, I'd shed a few because he wasn't with us now.

Big Ben struck the hour, and Kitten and Grandpop had a squabble about whether the New Year began on the first or last strokes of the hour. So they either saw the Old Year out with a quarrel, or they saw the New Year in with one, according to which one was right. But it didn't matter because their quarrels don't mean much anyhow, and soon they were all laughing and raising their glasses, and Puddy and Fionna rushed around the house, switching on all the lights so that everyone, even in Iona, would know they were bringing the New Year in!

And presently the telephone rang. It was Charlie

Bogilee, who had seen the lights, and wanted to give everyone a New Year greeting. Now Charlie lost both his legs in the First World War, and as he hasn't a telephone in his house, he had to go out to a call-box. This must have caused him a lot of trouble, and the family were all the more pleased with his greeting, because it wasn't easy for him to do it.

So instead of a first footer there had been a first telephoner, and everyone was very happy and ate some more shortbread and drank some more ginger wine before going to bed.

And the next morning, as Puddy let me into the house, I thought to myself, 'I am their first-footer, and I'm male. So it's lucky.' And though I didn't carry a coal, or any of the things that are customary when one is first-footing, I do hope I brought luck with me, just the same.

CHAPTER THIRTEEN

Margie and Lottie returned to London. Fionna returned to school. And the rain began. It rained and it rained, and the goats wouldn't leave their house because of the pools outside, so that Puddy, wearing gum boots and a mackintosh, had to go to them several times a day to feed them with hay and crushed oats, and to take them water.

She put a new mineral-lick in the container,

Nicholas

because perhaps it was boredom, or the kids they were expecting, that made the goats very eager to lick and lick at that red brick thing, which I had once tried and found horribly salty.

Grandpop was worrying in case the tons of lime he had ordered would arrive before Johnnie-the-Ploughman had been to plough the big field. Kitten blamed the rain for the fall in egg production, but she also blamed the hens, for she said it was time some of them were in the pot. Puddy made a few attempts at clearing up the garden, which was looking very battered and miserable, and which would look worse when the weeds began to grow. The rabbits had eaten the bark from the new apple bushes, which annoyed Puddy all the more because ever since the arrival of the polecat she had never managed to see a rabbit around at all.

The doctor's car often passed along the road, because there was a lot of influenza about, and sometimes the doctor came in to see the family, not because anyone was ill, but because he could have a hot cup of tea and a chat. And I often thought that he looked tired and could perhaps do with a doctor himself more than some of the people he visited.

Sometimes, in the evenings, the schoolteacher, who was a great friend of the family, came in bringing her knitting or her embroidery, both of which she did very well, and there would be a lot of chatter because the schoolteacher had travelled a great deal and had much to say of wonderful places. Places that I had read about in some of the books in the cottage, but never even hoped to see. It seemed to me a terrible shame that a clever person like that should have only six pupils in her school. But this was all part of what I said at the beginning, about the declining population, so I hope that those few children will grow up to appreciate the lovely place they live in and will find work to do here and rear huge families so that the tumble-down cottages will be built up and prosperity will be here once more. I am sure Arnish, who is so political, would know just how to bring this about.

At last, one day the rain stopped and the sun shone, and the puddles and the loch were covered in ice.

When I walked along the road to the village, I saw that Ben More, which is the highest mountain on Mull, was capped with snow. It is a strange thing, but we have a small hill near us, in the east, and because of this hill we can't see any of the mountains from the house. Curious, that what is so small can obliterate what is large. I suppose it is true of everything in life.

After a few days it was not only Ben More that was covered in snow. It was everything. And through the snow peeped the first shoots of the daffodils, and the robin redbreast who had hopped about outside the garage all winter now came right to the back door for his food. But the snow didn't lie long on the low ground, for it never does here, and one day Johnnie-the-Ploughman arrived with his tractor, so that Grandpop needn't have worried about the lime arriving too soon after all.

Puddy planted some willow cuttings inside the big field near the new gate which John had made. She thought these would help to soak up moisture from this wet corner of the field, and also that they would provide a windbreak. But Flora and Arnish soon slipped through that gate, which had been left open because of the ploughing, and they ate those lovely willows far faster than Puddy had planted them. And this, I thought, was unkind and unfeeling of them, but then, they are goats, whereas I am an affectionate cat that likes to please.

Of course, it must be remembered that soon their kids would be arriving, so perhaps the goats were not quite themselves. Puddy was still unsure if there were to be any kids, for it is extremely hard to tell with goats, but I knew because the goats knew. Only unfortunately I couldn't tell Puddy so.

Puddy, however, tells Carla everything, and so it was that I learnt that Corrie's foal was due next month, and that during the summer both Corrie and her foal were to be shown at the Royal Highland Show. And this time I was certain they would win first prize. Meanwhile Puddy busied herself repairing the boundaries of the paddock and making ready for Corrie's return home, and excitement tingled down my back, right to the very tips of my whiskers, as I thought how I would soon be seeing my best friend again!

All this time Kitten and Grandpop weren't idle. Kitten had made many, many pots of delicious marmalade, the smell of which had permeated the house for days. And Grandpop, humming his little hum (which wasn't about blessings any more), laid rat-traps in the barn, sorted Florrie once more and won thirty shillings in the pools.

And Carla, who at the age of four years, had not shown any interest in finding a mate, suddenly decided that she, too, would like a family, and she chose the coal-house, of all places, to make a nest. But I didn't take her very seriously. Time has taught me that where Carla is concerned, it's just a lot of bark.

One evening, when Johnnie-the-Postman came, Puddy gave him a letter to post, addressed to the poultry breeder in Stirling, from where she had bought last year's chicks. She was later in ordering them this year because of the wet weather. So soon another twittering box would be left at our gate by Neilachan, and I would probably be sitting on the wall when they arrived. Just like at the beginning of my book, which shows how, in the country, the wheel most surely goes full circle.

But before the chickens arrived, news came of the death of dear, cosy little Miss Sarah, who lived with her dear, cosy little sisters in a house by the sea, a few miles away. All the family loved Miss Sarah and her sisters, and as the weather was too cold for Grandpop to attend the funeral, Puddy went instead.

When Puddy returned, she said it was the loveliest funeral she had ever been to. And she described it so that I can write about it just as if I had been there myself, and I do understand, just as I hope you will, why she called it a lovely funeral, which seems such a peculiar thing to say.

When she arrived at the house where Miss Sarah had lived, one of Miss Sarah's sisters greeted her and took her into the parlour, where there was tea to drink and plenty of sandwiches and cakes. And while Puddy sipped her tea, Miss Sarah's sister looked through the window at the blue sky and at the sun shining on the daffodils and sparkling on the blue sea at the bottom of the garden, and she said, in her lovely soft Highland voice, 'It's a wonderful thing, but Sarah said only the other day that she always gets lovely weather whenever she does a journey.'

And presently Puddy, and all the other people who had gathered, were asked to go out into the garden, and there they found Sarah's coffin, placed on two chairs outside the front door she had so often used all her life. The coffin was piled high with daffodils, and Puddy kept her eyes on these, as the Minister said the burial service and led the singing of the twenty-third psalm to the tune of Crimond. And all the time the sea lapped and foamed at the bottom of the garden, and Miss Sarah's cosy sisters kept their chins up high, fortified in their knowledge that Sarah loved this sunny travelling day.

Then the coffin was carried shoulder-high to the waiting lorry, which had superseded the old farm cart as a hearse, and Puddy got into Florrie and followed the cortege for miles and miles over an incredibly bumpy road until the burial ground was reached: a burial ground hidden right away among the mountains and so ancient that the bones of the very earliest Scottish Christians must be buried there.

The grave was already dug. The coffin was lowered into it, and, after a brief prayer, the earth was piled back over it. Finally a trim green carpet of turf, which had been carefully dug away, was neatly rolled over the brown soil like a cosy, green blanket. And it was patted into place by the gravedigger, whose work-worn hands now had the gentleness of a woman's. Then the wreaths were arranged over the grave, and the funeral was over. Only the long, difficult drive home remained.

'It wasn't like an end. It was like a beginning,' Puddy said, adding rather unnecessarily, 'like planting a bulb.'

And that is why I have chosen the funeral as the last episode in my book, because life goes on and on, no matter what end, seemingly, we come to.

A blackbird is singing his heart out from a chimney stack. Grandpop is humming a hum as he makes sure that the paddock boundaries will hold against the onslaught of an inquisitive foal. Puddy is in the cottage clearing a place for the brooder, where she will rear the day-old chicks. Kitten is preparing Margie's and Fionna's bedrooms in readiness for the Easter holidays. And Carla has promised she will not allow Lottie to romp with the goats, since their kids will soon be born. And on the mantelpiece in the drawing-room is an airmail letter from John, saying that he has been posted back to Britain, so he'll be home on leave, and please to lay out lots of FOOD.

As for me, I am kept busy visiting my families, hunting and writing my memoirs, for I realise that, with so much yet to happen, there's no telling when my memories will end. So maybe there will come a day when this will appear on your bookshelves, printed on India paper, vellum bound and bearing the words 'Volume One' in gilded capitals on the spine. Who knows?

Afterword

Nicholas recorded his observations during the early 1950s while Puddy, in addition to milking goats and tending hens, started to write a romantic novel and consigned the works of Nicholas to a drawer, where they remained for nearly sixty years.

Many changes occurred on Mull during that time. Mains electricity followed by water on tap transformed the Ross of Mull. The road was upgraded, although still single track, and the long awaited pier was built at Craignure. The picturesque motor boats which plied between Mull and Iona were replaced by an ungainly but practical ferry conveying many more foot passengers, while benefiting the island farmers.

Despite these improvements, the population continued to dwindle and the primary school closed in the 1970s. The granite building, which always served as venue for community events, thus became the village hall. Then a gradual change brought increased tourism and a level of prosperity. Incomers seeking the simple life restored tumbled-down cottages and developed holiday homes. New houses were built, and even the old church, once used as a byre, became a dwelling house. Meanwhile, descendants of that easy-going generation which willingly supported the family through thick and thin formed the bedrock of the community.

On the domestic front, the goats produced four kids between them, while Corrieshellach gave birth to a filly and won first prize in her class at the Royal Highland Show. Over the years Puddy – Annabel Carothers – wrote two more romantic novels which, combined as a trilogy, became *Kilcaraig*, published in 1982. If Nicholas recorded Volume II of his memoirs, there is no trace of it. He died peacefully at Achaban House and was buried in the garden.

Fionna Eden-Bushell
February 2010